GOING ROGUE

THE COMPILATION

Kerry Patton

Quiet Owl Books

GOING ROGUE
THE COMPILATION

Copyright © 2013 Kerry Patton

ISBN-13: 978-0-9898331-5-8

All rights reserved. Except for quotations for articles and reviews, no part of this book may be reproduced or transmitted in any form or by any means without written permission from the author. The views expressed in this work are solely those of the author and do not reflect the views of the publisher, and the publisher hereby disclaims any responsibility for them.

To request a review copy for an article or to interview the author, please email press@quietowl.com.

Cover Design by Jennifer Welker

Published by Quiet Owl Books
quietowl.com

Quiet Owl Books are available for bulk purchases at special discounts for schools, organizations, and special events. For more information, please contact books@quietowl.com.

Read more about Kerry Patton at:
Kerry-Patton.com
QuietOwl.com/Kerry-Patton

Disclaimer: This book was inspired by world events and, in many ways, current conspiracies. However, it is a work of fiction. All the characters in this book are also completely fictitious. To the best of the author's understanding, it is not known whether any specific classified device noted in this book exists. Again, this book is a work of fiction and should be considered as such.

About the Author

Kerry Patton is an internationally recognized security, terrorism, and intelligence professional. He has taught domestic and international organizations in counter-terrorism, intelligence, and physical security related issues. He has briefed some of the highest government officials ranging from ambassadors and members of Congress and Pentagon staff.

Kerry has served his country honorably throughout South America, Africa, the Middle East, Asia, and Europe, fulfilling human intelligence and physical security operations. He has conducted risk management programs on critical assets, carried out tactical surveys of more than five hundred international airfields and energy platforms, and supported in the protection of Afghan President Karzai. While operating in some of today's most classified US government programs, Kerry has interviewed (outside of interrogations) terrorists and former terrorists within multiple groups, which include Hezb Islami Gullbidine, Taliban, Maoist rebels, and the Palestinian Liberation Organization. He operated in and outside of Afghanistan from 2001 through late 2008. His knowledge of Afghanistan has been shared through numerous speaking venues from radio talk shows, academic conferences, and law enforcement seminars, to non-public government engagements.

Kerry serves as the vice president of training and public relations for the Emerald Society of the Federal Law Enforcement Agencies. He currently teaches counter-terrorism, intelligence, and protection management courses for Henley-Putnam University.

A Special Thank You

To all the men and women who endured the horrors at war and continue to suffer, you are not alone. Our veterans deserve the best considering the sacrifices they have made for each and every one of us and our nation. This compilation of shorts is an attempt to enlighten the American public and expose the issues some of our veterans deal with on a daily basis.

It is sad but true that some of our veterans have been misdiagnosed and over prescribed medications that actually do more harm than good in helping them in their daily lives. The effects of some of these drugs are startling.

There is access to some exceptional organizations willing to assist our veterans in need. One of those organizations is the Valhalla Project. I support the Valhalla Project knowing what it does, how it is managed, and understanding how the organization is a 100% volunteer military friendly non-profit organization—no volunteer is paid unlike many non-profit organizations.

To learn more about the Valhalla Project, please go to their website and check them out.

http://www.valhalla-project.com/

They thought they knew me…
They thought they could use me…
They thought they could abuse me…
But they never knew a thing about me…
I am Nathan Belovich, and payback is a bitch…

EPISODE ONE

Nathan Belovich walked into the classroom for the first time. With a briefcase, wired glasses, and a blue pinstriped suit, he dressed the part. This would be his first class teaching advanced computer science at NYU.

"I do not take roll call," Nathan said and placed his briefcase on the podium. "If you are here, good. If you're not here, that's your loss."

The students began to chuckle under their breaths.

"I am here to teach you everything I know about computers." Nathan stared out at the class. "I will teach you everything I know from years of working for the world's largest technology manipulators…the NSA."

"You're a spy?" one of the brunette females, wearing a slutty plaid miniskirt, muttered.

"I was a spy."

Nathan obtained the attention he desired. He was direct, not withholding his background from his students. He needed them to trust him.

"In this course, you can do what you wish, but if you do what I ask, you will become some of the most astute technicians in the computer world." Nathan turned his back toward the students, walked to his briefcase, and pulled out a small device with a USB connector attached.

"What is that?"

"This, my friends, is worth more than any amount of gold you could possibly carry."

"Yeah, but what is it?" the girl in the miniskirt asked.

"What is your name, miss?"

"Karen," she replied.

"This, Karen, can get you more power than the president of the United States."

"How so?" Karen uncrossed her legs, leaning forward against her desk with great inquisitiveness.

"If I told you this little device could get you into every major bank, every major news network, every major political office, would you believe me?"

"Is that some type of sniffer device?" a young black student asked from the back of the room.

"What is your name?" Nathan asked.

"Jerome. My name is Jerome."

"No, Jerome." Nathan walked toward the middle of the room, assessing his students. "This is unlike anything known to the public. This is a wireless device that can infiltrate the most secured networks in the world and capture anything I instruct it to retrieve."

"Isn't that illegal?" Karen sounded confused.

"I used one of these recently on Americans, per the instruction of my former employer. Are you suggesting I'm a criminal?" Nathan asked.

Karen did not reply.

"Your first lesson is understanding that the government has been spying on you ever since you were brought into this world. Your second lesson is knowing that with technology forever advancing, US laws are lagging behind. And third, acknowledging that everyone is responsible for their own network's security. That includes every one of you, every major corporation, and every political office."

Jerome's pearly white teeth shone with a smile. "Are you going to teach us how to use that?"

"That's up to you, Jerome." Nathan smirked. "Would you like to know how to use it?"

The bulk of the class nodded, excluding Karen, who still looked overwhelmed and confused.

"How would you like to play a little trick on the students here on campus and on the entire NYU faculty?"

Nathan opened his laptop and plugged it into the system, which controlled the overhead projector. On the large screen he showed his class the needed steps to *have fun*. After connecting the device to the USB port, then typing some characters for all to see, he stopped and looked up at his students.

"If I told you that in the next forty-five seconds, the entire campus will have a blackout, would you believe me?"

He left the podium and began to walk between the desks where his students sat.

"Twenty seconds."

"Is this for real?" Jerome asked.

"No way," a young Asian male, who sat beside Jerome, blurted.

"What was your name?" Nathan asked.

"Peter. Peter Yon."

"Ten seconds," Nathan noted.

"Five seconds," Jerome added.

"Four," the class began to count down.

"Three."

"Two."

"One."

The classroom succumbed to complete darkness. The computers in the room shut down. All electricity within the building went out.

"You see, my friends…" Nathan paused and took a slow breath. "…that tool can be the one tool that changes the world."

"Sir, my computer isn't plugged into any electrical outlet, but it too shut down," Peter, the squirrely Asian, informed Nathan.

"I never said anything about having to be connected to an electrical source, did I?" Nathan asked with a grin.

A minute passed, and prior to the classroom lapsing into hysteria, the lights and power turned back on, along with Peter's computer.

Peter and Jerome were in disbelief, as was the rest of the class. Karen remained confused.

"I've heard about something called a HERF device. Is that what this thing is?" Peter asked.

"High Energy Radio Frequency…" Nathan blurted and observed Peter's facial non-communications. "Some may assume this is a HERF device, but they would only be partially correct. There is so much more to this device, so much more to its abilities, so much more, only one person in the world truly understands."

"And who would that person be?" Karen questioned with an attitude.

"Me."

"So you created it?" she asked.

"When the government needs something unique, they bring specialists like me into a playing field few others understand," Nathan explained.

"I'm confused." Jerome chuckled innocently to disguise his anxiety.

"Has anyone here ever heard of the Defense Advanced Research Projects Agency or the Intelligence Advanced Research Projects Activity?"

Some of the students nodded, showing their knowledge of both entities, while many sat as still as rocks.

"These are two research organizations inside the darkest corners of the United States government," Nathan explained. "Those that work in these organizations create special items on request. Sometimes, though, the government doesn't like the end result. So, they scratch the program altogether."

"Is that what happened to your project?" Peter asked and began to reboot his laptop. "Why wouldn't the government want something like this?"

Nathan didn't answer Peter's question. He simply moved on with the lesson. "Are there any more questions?"

"You said it wasn't just a HERF device." Jerome raised an eyebrow. "What else can it do?"

"What do you want it to do?"

"Yeah, Jerome, what more do you want it to do?" Karen snarkily remarked.

"Peter, let me know when your computer is back up," Nathan said. "Once it's up, open up whatever e-mail system you use. I will show you something."

"It's up."

Nathan went back to the podium and typed some characters on the key pad of his computer, projecting his screen on the wall for the entire class to see. "Wait for it….Ahhh…Here we go."

Within seconds, Nathan displayed the same e-mail system Peter had on his own computer. Every name of every person in his inbox was revealed, along with every message's title. The students were shocked.

"It gets better." Nathan typed some more. "I now can open any e-mail of yours and actually read it. I could even respond to e-mails if I wished. No one would know it was me; everyone would believe my responses came directly from you."

Nathan opened an e-mail to demonstrate he was not lying.

"Mr. Belovich, there must be some type of legality issue behind using that thing." Karen, with a sharp eye, looked at her new professor.

"So you're my legal guardian?" Nathan asked then smiled at the room.

"I just think some type of law against it must be out there," Karen explained. "I mean, imagine if that got into the hands of the wrong person. They could destroy all of America, if they wanted to."

"Precisely."

A few students rustled as they began packing their belongings. Nathan looked at his watch and realized class was over.

"Enjoy your day, folks," Nathan said. "And, remember, you never know who is watching you."

Peter and Jerome rushed toward the front of the room where Nathan was standing. Karen was nearby, slow to pack her things.

"Mr. Belovich, on Thursdays at 7:00 pm, a group of us meet at Think Coffee," Jerome said. "It's right down the block from the Courant Institute of Mathematical Sciences. Come out there tomorrow."

"Yeah, it's between Third and Fourth Streets," Peter chimed in. "You can't miss it. You should come out tomorrow night and just observe some of the things we're trying to do."

"Oh, that's great." Karen stood, revealing her thigh-high miniskirt and knee-high black stockings. "The last thing you guys need is for a computer wizard like Mr. Belovich to help you with your Occupy Wall Street nonsense."

Nathan chuckled. "I appreciate the offer, but Karen is right. You don't need me to be involved in that type of thing."

"No, Mr. Belovich." Jerome shunned Karen by turning his back to her. "Don't listen to her. We aren't involved with that. We're just a bunch of computer geeks that get together and try to find ways to advance ourselves."

"Yeah, it's like a brainstorming session," Peter added. "We're looking for grants, but we have to come together to find what is really needed in computer technology research first. And you know what is needed. Maybe you can help us."

"No Occupy nonsense?" Nathan asked.

"We promise."

Karen, with her hazel eyes, beamed up at Nathan. "What is it the Russians always say? Trust but verify?"

"So you know Russian intelligence?" Nathan looked a little surprised.

"My father."

"Your father was Russian intelligence?" Nathan asked.

"No. He's FBI," she said. "I learned some foreign intelligence mottos from him."

"Which is why you kept pushing about the legal issues that come with the tool I showed in class?" Nathan began to passively elicit.

"I want to get into the FBI when I graduate," Karen explained. "I'm specifically trying to get into cybercrime."

"Follow your father's footsteps." Nathan smiled. "I am sure he'll be overly proud of you."

"No," Karen interrupted. "He's not in cybercrime. He works foreign intelligence. Mostly for the United Nations."

"Karen, if there is anything I can ever help with to make your career dream come true, please don't hesitate to ask."

Karen smiled at Nathan for the first time. It was obvious she had felt somewhat at ease throughout the short conversation.

"Well, Mr. Belovich, what do you say?" Jerome cut in. "You coming tomorrow or what?"

"Yeah, sir," Peter added. "We really could use you."

Nathan looked at Karen, winked, and answered the two men. "Only if Karen goes too. I always like to have a second set of eyes around to make sure I'm not being lured into something that can potentially bite me in the ass."

"What do you say, Karen?" Jerome asked.

"Yeah, come on," Peter blurted. "You have never been out there with us, but you always suggest we're up to no good. It's about time you see for yourself."

"Yeah, and plus, a bunch of geeks like us always look a lot cooler with a woman hanging around," Jerome noted and laughed.

"At the first sign of one of you losers hitting on me, I walk," Karen warned.

"No one will hit on you," Nathan said. "I'll keep them in line."

"What do you say?" Jerome demanded.

"See you guys tomorrow evening," Karen said, confirming the date.

"I need to get going." Nathan turned to his desk to begin collecting his things. "You three behave. We are a team. No infighting."

"See you later, Mr. Belovich," they all muttered.

Karen walked out of the building and toward her car, grabbed her keys, and opened the door. She sat in the parking lot for a moment, thinking about the class and Mr. Belovich. After she reached into her purse, she pulled out her phone to make a call.

"Daddy, it's me."

"Hey, sweetie, how's your day going?"

"Met my new professor," Karen began. "Says he was with the NSA. Then he mentioned something about DARPA and IARPA and his workings with those two organizations. Does that make any sense to you?"

"Those are three really secretive organizations, hun. Sounds like you have an incredibly fascinating teacher this semester. What a way to wrap up the last class you need before graduation, wouldn't you say?"

"Something about the guy just didn't sit well with me, Daddy."

"I'm sure he's a fine professor." Her father was comforting. "He's a former spook. Of course he doesn't sit right with you. But I'm sure you will see in time, he is a good man trying to assist in any way he can."

"Well, I'm going out with some of the class tomorrow night at seven at Think Coffee." Karen wanted her father to know where she would be. "Mr. Belovich will be there with us."

"See, it sounds like he really is going to be proactive in helping everyone out."

"Daddy, he showed us something today I think you should know about."

"What was it?"

"Some computer gadget with a plug-in adaptor for a USB drive." Karen looked through her front window at the surrounding cars. No one walked through the parking lot. She was alone. "He shut down the school's electrical grid, but more interesting than that, he was able to shut down people's computers even though they weren't plugged into any outlets."

"He brought a HERF device into the school?"

"No, and it wasn't some unique form of a HERF device either." Karen continued, "Later in the class, he was able to go into another student's e-mail and actually read it as if he were sitting behind the student's laptop."

10

The phone went silent for a minute.

"Karen, you're going to meet with this professor of yours tomorrow night?" Karen's father didn't wait for a response before he offered his instructions: "Try to learn more about this device. Try to learn as much as you can about this professor. But make sure you are completely harmless in doing this."

"OK, Daddy." Karen confirmed her willingness. "I will see you over the weekend, OK?"

"OK. I love you, sweetie."

"Love you too, Daddy."

A sudden knock thumped against Karen's car door. It startled her, forcing her phone to bumble out of her hand and through her legs, onto the seat's upholstery. Her miniskirt was too short to catch the phone and keep it on her lap. She looked up with fright.

It was Nathan Belovich, waving goodbye as he journeyed through the parking lot and headed to his vehicle.

"Hope you don't stand us up tomorrow!" he blurted loud enough so that she could hear him through the car's window.

"I won't."

•••

Large chalk boards covered with cursive multi-colored chalk, divulging the specialty of the day, stood on display near the counter. Glass jars filled with an array of biscotti cookies rested near the cash register. An assortment of knick-knacks for purchase, like coffee cups and T-shirts, hung close by. It was a typical coffee shop, and it didn't thrill Nathan in the least.

"Cappuccino," Nathan requested from the barista.

He turned and looked at all the college-aged hipsters working like bees high on caffeine. Nathan saw Jerome and Peter, along with a few of their associates, sitting on metal chairs across from each other. Their laptops were open on the table.

With coffee in hand, he walked toward them.

"Hey, Mr. B!" Jerome stood and greeted his professor. "Nice to see you made it!"

"What are we working on, gents?"

"Just looking through DARPA's website, searching for some defense solicitations," Peter responded.

"Ah, so you men do listen." Nathan grinned.

"When you said you once worked closely with DARPA and IARPA, we figured, maybe, that was the best way we could seek some federal grants," Jerome added as he settled onto the industrial-looking chair.

"Take a look at their information innovation and microsystems technology offices. You might find some interesting things there. It'll be a good start." Nathan pointed to the side of the web page once Jerome had opened it on his computer.

All eyes immediately turned toward the front door of the coffee shop. Her wavy hair swept down her back, her legs showed the skin below her thighs, and her wardrobe made her look like a high-class gothic call girl. It was Karen.

"Leather mini, jet-black lipstick, metal in your face..." Peter jovially described Karen's appearance. "Going to Gotham City for a date with Batman later tonight?"

"That's it, I'm out of here." Karen spun away from the group.

"He's only joking." Nathan reached for Karen's arm. "Remember, guys like Peter don't get to hang around attractive, free-spirited women often, so he didn't know how to thank you for showing up."

"Whatever." Karen's attitude was evident, but she revealed her appeasement when she looked down at Nathan's hand, and didn't pull away. "Anyway…so, Mr. Belovich, are you our professor tonight or are you one of us?"

"Why do you ask?" Nathan let go of Karen. "Never mind. I am one of you."

Karen smiled, but it was a smile Nathan knew to be cautious of. Something wasn't right with Karen. He sensed it during class. And he was sensing it now. But in his world, life was filled with games and he knew all too well how to play most of them.

"That thing you had today…" Karen began, and straddled a nearby chair, showing as much leg as possible without revealing her panties…if she was even wearing any, Nathan thought. "Why do you have it and not the government?"

"Universities do a lot of research for the government," Nathan explained while noticing, yet not revealing that he was paying any attention to Karen's slutty movements. "A lot of the items universities create per government grants are never accepted as final products, so they stay with the university."

"And the last one you worked for allowed you to keep that?" she continued her interrogation.

"Who says I was working for any university? I was working with a university on the project. Working with and working for are two totally separate animals. I was the lead government representative. I monitored everything they did. My colleagues didn't believe SAM was worthy enough to incorporate into active service."

"SAM?" Jerome asked.

"That's the name of the device," Nathan explained. "Synthetic Acquisition Master."

"Acquisition? As in…to collect?" Peter muttered.

"Ah, but as you saw with the temporary blackout, it has the ability to do much more than that."

"I just don't understand what it's for." Karen leaned back in the chair to look up at her professor, who stood beside her.

"When the Arab Spring evolved in Egypt…" Nathan began to divulge as he looked down, his eyes confronted with Karen's full cleavage. "…many analysts believed social media like Twitter played a significant role, and it did. But a small team of Americans were in Cairo at the beginning of the protests. They were the ones who helped start the riots in Cairo. They did this by using SAM."

"I just don't get it." Jerome's expression began to match Karen's.

"They used SAM to tap into thousands of Twitter accounts based in Cairo." Nathan continued, finally taking a seat. "Once they captured the Twitter accounts of those they knew had specific followings, they created false tweets that looked like they came from the owner. Those tweets helped fuel everything that occurred. It was a live pilot program."

"So this device took over an entire country and helped replace a nation's government?" Peter was impressed and sat back in his chair with amazement.

"Not really," Nathan countered. "SAM simply helped facilitate everything. Once the ball started to roll, SAM wasn't needed any longer."

"That's scary," Karen said. "So in reality, the revolt in Egypt was a US-led initiative, which used college kids like us."

"What was scary was when my three students were held by authorities for several days against their will. Luckily, one of them was the son of a US diplomat."

"Wait a second." Jerome was slightly startled and closed his laptop. "I remember hearing about those students. You're saying they were actually there to test SAM?"

"Precisely."

"No," Peter interjected. "They weren't there just to test SAM. They were there to do a job I thought the CIA always did. You know, overthrow governments."

"And our government approved this mission in Egypt?" Karen didn't appreciate what she was hearing. "They approved of a few college kids going abroad and actually testing this device on a country, knowing if it worked, Egypt's government would be overthrown?"

"Let's just say that the US government wanted SAM tested." Nathan paused and sipped his coffee. "Specific tasks needed to be accomplished….objectives mandated by the United States."

"You didn't really answer the question," Karen blurted.

"Sure I did." Nathan smiled. "You just didn't like what you heard."

"Oh, snap!" Jerome shouted and placed his fist before his mouth. "You two are like a married couple!"

"He wishes." Karen looked at Nathan and smiled. "I saw him checking me out earlier."

"How could anyone not check you out with what you're wearing?" Nathan laughed. "You were doing it intentionally so we could all see what you wanted us to see."

"Yeah, you are a tease, Karen," Peter noted.

"All this sexual frustration…" Nathan chuckled. "I'm headed to the Bleecker Street Bar."

"Wait a second. You're leaving us?" Jerome asked. "You can't leave now. I want to know more about how this Egypt thing really happened."

"I told you all…our government is fucked up!" Peter shut his computer in disbelief. "Our government is willing to use college kids to do its dirty work."

"You think this is the first time the government's used college kids?" Karen asked.

Nathan knew he had sparked the minds at the table. He sensed Peter and Jerome distrusted the government, yet where Karen stood remained unclear. It was time to leave.

"While I enjoy the company, I am a scotch man." Nathan placed his coffee on the table.

"I love a good scotch and cigar." Karen stood.

"Would never have guessed." Nathan furrowed his brow. "I would have taken you for a Bud Light type of woman."

"Any of you losers coming?" Karen looked at her geeky peers.

"Not twenty-one," Peter replied.

"I don't drink." Jerome remained seated.

"Looks like it's just you and me, Professor." Karen smiled and placed her hand on Nathan's elbow, suggesting they leave.

"I think you better stay here."

"What?" Karen asked and brushed shoulders with the elder of the two. "You scared to be out with little old me?"

"As I said..." Nathan gently eased Karen down on the empty chair. "It takes some time to acquire the taste of a good scotch...How old are you?"

"Old enough to know that when I like something, I get it." Karen snickered.

"That reminds me of something I'd expect to hear from some Jersey housewife...not some college-aged girl."

"Maybe I'm a bit more mature than the average college girl."

Nathan placed his hand on Karen's shoulder to indicate his goodbye. He then walked around the table where Peter and Jerome, along with a few others, were sitting and shook their hands.

"Will see you all back in class."

•••

Nathan turned and walked out of the coffee shop as a light rain dripped out of the night sky. It took but a few minutes to walk toward Bleecker Street Bar located between Lafayette and Broadway. He walked in the bar and liked what he saw. Few patrons, wood all around giving it that old school feel, a few pool tables, and some dartboards.

"Dewar's." Nathan asked the bartender for his scotch of choice and claimed one of the many empty barstools.

"How you want that?" the skinny forty-something-year-old male behind the bar asked in his thick New York accent.

"Doesn't matter." Nathan turned to the nearby television, which was airing the Yankees. "Just want something to quench my thirst."

He abandoned his stool and walked toward the back of the bar where two restroom doors were adjacent to one another, along with a third door. He perched it open to see what was behind it. It led to an alley outside of the watering hole. He spotted a dumpster only feet from the door. As he looked up, he noticed a security camera system pointed downward. Situational awareness was something Nathan appreciated. And no matter where he went, he always found an alternative exit.

Upon returning to his seat, Nathan saw a small rock glass waiting for him, filled with his brown water. He picked it up, smelled the contents within, and placed the glass near his lips. Before he could taste the beverage, a subtle commotion made him turn to observe.

"Oh shit," he said, spying the one person he wished not to see enter the bar.

"Hey, Karen!" the bartender shouted. "Thought you were off tonight."

"Just came in to have a drink," Karen noted and sat on an empty bar stool near her professor. Nathan pretended not to see his student. He played it as though the two had never met.

"I'll have what he's having."

"Dewar's?" He looked confused. "I got your Macallan's tucked away for you. You sure you don't want that?"

Karen turned to look at Nathan. "Thought you said you were a scotch man. That crap isn't scotch."

"It suits me just fine right now."

"Brian, I'll take my Macallan's."

"Work here?"

"Two years now."

"Like it?" Nathan allowed his index finger to run over the rim of the glass sitting in front of him.

"The guys take good care of me."

The conversation was put on hold as Karen received her drink. Nathan continued watching the Yankees on the flat screen. He grew bored, realizing his glass was almost dry.

"You're not a real professor, are you?" Karen turned and looked at Nathan with drink in hand.

"Don't even have a PhD," Nathan responded, turning his eyes to the television. "I was asked to come here solely based off my past life."

"First gig away from the agency?"

"Kind of."

"What do you mean?" Karen sipped her drink.

"I was assigned at MIT prior to this. Not as a professor but as an observer." Nathan turned his head and looked at his drink, staring into the reflection. "The things those kids are capable of achieving is more than impressive."

"I heard the government gives out a lot of grants to those at MIT."

"Grants?" Nathan chuckled. "When it comes to technological advancements, I've found the government relentlessly uses those kids for things they often don't have any clue about. If only the students really knew what they were doing, what they were creating, and how it would eventually be used."

"And that upsets you?"

"Upset me?" Nathan finished off his drink and signaled the bartender for a refill. "They never obtained security clearances, were never let in on reality. They are innocent. Yet the government uses them. Don't you believe that's a bit immoral?"

"A man with a conscience."

"Was told long ago not to think." Nathan reached forward to embrace his refill. "How do they expect anyone to turn off their cognitive processes? How does the government expect people to simply turn blind eyes?"

"Which is why you left and decided to work at NYU?"

Nathan didn't verbally respond. He swirled the liquid inside his glass and slightly nodded. He watched the liquid spin like an inverted tornado. The liquid resembled how he felt mentally.

"You're a smart guy, Nathan." Karen suggested another drink. "Be careful in your transition. You know a lot."

Karen's remark sparked Nathan's attention, yet he did not show it. "If I wanted to become another Bradley Manning or Edward Snowden, I could have leaked thousands of documents. I would never do that. That's cowardly. I'm a level-headed professional."

"Well, what do you think so far?" Karen wished to move on to the more current thoughts that may have been running through Nathan's mind as she received her refill. "What do you think of NYU? The students? It must be very different from MIT."

"What is there to think about?" Nathan showed his glass to Brian, the bartender, requesting another. "I had to think a lot in my career. I'm tired of thinking right now."

"You're lying." Karen gently grabbed Nathan by the elbow, forcing him to look at her.

Nathan turned and looked into Karen's eyes. He wanted to laugh, knowing how right she was, but he could never give her the upper hand.

"You mentioned something the other day about Jerome and Peter being a part of the Occupy Wall Street movement…Were you serious?" Nathan asked and reached for his glass.

"You don't care about those two." Karen swallowed her drink. "Or do you?"

Sensing a shift in the air, Nathan asked, "What do you want from me?"

Karen giggled, placed her hand on his thigh, and leaned closer. She brought her lips next to his ear, then whispered. "Your cock."

She then grabbed his hand and slid it up her bare thigh. "You want me, Mr. Belovich. I know you do. And I am here. Just you and me. I know you want to fuck this little school girl."

Nathan gently took his hand off Karen's leg and turned, facing the bar where his glass of scotch rested. He took the glass and swallowed all of its contents in one large gulp. "What would you think if I told you I was gay?" After placing the empty glass on the wooden bar, he stood and walked toward the bathroom.

Karen jumped off her barstool and stopped Nathan in his tracks, only feet from the bathroom door.

"You go in there, I'm following you."

Nathan didn't respond and continued on. Karen followed. "If you really are gay, I'm going to make you straight."

Nathan opened the bathroom door and took a few steps inward. Karen was right behind him. He quickly turned as the door shut. His hand grabbed Karen by the neck. Her eyes widened.

"Now fuck me," Nathan quietly demanded.

Her hands quickly unzipped his pants. Nathan hiked her skirt up around her waist. Panties were not worn. After massaging him to a full erection, Karen inserted what she longed for.

Nathan placed his hand behind her knee, forcing her leg around his waist. In position, he did the same with her other leg, holding onto her ass now that both legs were wrapped around him.

He quickly moved both bodies, as one, into the nearest stall. There, he forced her body against its walls and lunged himself deeper and deeper inside her as she groaned with each thrust. With each hard jolt, the act became more violent. Karen's bodily fluids soaked inside her.

Nathan's breath grew deeper and deeper as he continued to thrust. Karen moaned in his ear, quiet enough so no one in the bar could hear. Nathan could not hold on any longer and burst deep inside her.

"Are you fucking kidding me?" she exclaimed as she attempted to catch some much needed air. "You just came inside me?"

"Would I be the first to come inside you?" Nathan asked as he zipped his pants, opened the stall door, and exited the bathroom, leaving Karen behind.

His night was coming to a close, and to evade the drama that would come after fucking some slut, he reached for some cash out of his wallet and placed it on the bar. Without stopping, he exited the watering hole and headed back to his apartment.

•••

A loud burst sounded by the apartment door, which swung open faster than lightning strikes. Nathan jumped off the sofa in an attempt to gain some distance from the threat that had startled him. He was stopped in his tracks by the steel pointed at his head.

"Don't you fucking move," the tall, well-built stranger said with his weapon aimed.

Nathan raised his hands. "Who are you?"

"Your worst nightmare." He grabbed Nathan's wrist and swung him to the ground.

"A cop," Nathan blurted and braced himself for the knee he knew would eventually land on the small of his back. It wasn't the first he was apprehended, and he knew police restraint tactics. "You must be Karen's father."

A sudden blow connected with the back of Nathan's head.

"Shut the fuck up."

Nathan lay motionless. He could feel the warm liquid trickle on his ear.

"You raped my daughter." He began to zip-tie Nathan's hands behind his back.

Nathan chuckled for a brief second. "Is that what she told you? That I raped her?"

Nathan felt a hand on the back of his head. No sooner, his skull slammed into the floor.

"You're going to tell me everything," Karen's father said as he rolled Nathan to his back. "I'm going to ask you a series of questions, and you're gonna nod either yes or no. Do you understand me?"

Nathan nodded, showing he understood as Karen's father shoved the muzzle of his pistol into Nathan's mouth.

"Are you Nathan Belovich? Is that your real name?"

Nathan nodded.

"Karen showed me the marks on her neck. They were from your hand, correct?"

Nathan again nodded, yes. No sooner, he felt a blunt strike hit his face. His eye began to swell. Another strike landed in the same spot. Two blows back to back, and Nathan realized this was going to be a long night.

The gun moved away from Nathan's mouth. He was raised to his feet and pulled across the small New York City apartment and into the kitchen area where two metal seats rested around a tiny kitchen table. Karen's father slammed him onto one of the chairs, his hands still behind his back. He felt them being tied to the chair, preventing his escape.

"Did she tell you how she followed me into the bathroom? Did she tell you that the bartender watched us go into the bathroom?" Nathan looked up at his interrogator.

"That bartender was an off-duty FBI agent, a friend." Karen's father began searching the premise. "Wait a second. She followed you into the bathroom?"

"Do you really believe a friend of yours would allow a guy like me, a guy he had never seen before, just grab your daughter and pull her into the bathroom?" Nathan asked as he stared down at the linoleum. It was a sign of passiveness.

Another blow assaulted Nathan's head. "Your story is not going to save your ass. I know you followed her to the rear exit of the bar. I know what you did to her next to the dumpster. I have the photos."

"You don't have any photos." Nathan looked at his assailant and tasted the iron in his bleeding mouth.

"I don't, huh?" The weapon-toting man pulled out his cell phone and showed Nathan a picture of Karen lying next to a dumpster, alone.

"Who are you?" Nathan glanced at the photo. "What's your name?"

"Call me Sam." He placed the phone back in his pocket. "You like that name, don't you?…Sam."

"You're not with the FBI." Nathan realized he'd been set up.

"I'm not with the FBI?" Sam asked and pulled the second chair in front of Nathan. "Then who am I with?"

Nathan leaned back in his seat. Blood trickled out of his mouth as he half smiled. "Synthetic Acquisition Master. You're the human form of SAM. That's why you chose that name. That's why you refused to give me your real name. Used what I knew. Used a name I could relate to. Was that a personal decision, or did one of your handlers instruct you to use that name?"

"I extract a lot of information from pukes like you." Sam, with his stomach facing the back of the chair, sat. "I have used extraction methods all my life. And you, my friend, will tell me everything I want."

Nathan shook his head left and right. "I think you have mistaken me for some terrorist you possibly interrogated in some CIA black site."

"We'll see about that." Sam stood and began to walk toward the counter where Nathan's cutlery set was located.

"If you kill me, America will implode with a revolution…a revolution much bloodier than America's first," Nathan said and glared across the room and into the living room where the encounter had begun.

His statement startled Sam, who quickly turned to Nathan. "Explain."

"Let's get some things straight first." Nathan turned the tide of the interrogation. "Is Karen really your daughter?"

"Fuck you."

"Will you accept the fact that I never raped her and accept that I was set up?"

Sam paused and wondered how much Nathan really knew. He paced toward Nathan and sat once again.

"I know who you are, what your mission is, why you are here," Nathan said with his one good eye directed at Sam. "And I prepared for this."

Sam shook the foreboding thoughts from his mind and did his best to reenter the role he was sent to fulfill. "You have no clue who I am." He grabbed Nathan's hair and pulled his head back. "Where is it?"

"Where is what?"

"Where is the device?"

"I can tell you that it's not in the ceiling and it isn't in this building." Nathan felt the pressure in his head release.

"Then where?"

"Which one?" Nathan smiled. "Oh, you were told there's only one device?…Those who sent you here are idiots."

"No, no, no…" Sam shook his head in protest. "Only one was built. We know this."

"Wrong."

"Then how many?"

"More than your folks wanted." Nathan glanced at Sam's pocket where he heard a phone vibrate. "Gonna answer that? Could it be your female counterpart, who I fucked earlier?" Another blow targeted Nathan, and he shook away the pain as much as possible. "Tell me the truth. Karen isn't your daughter. She is a counterpart of yours. You two were banging one another, weren't you? You got jealous tonight, which is why you're doing this job with such violence. You know it doesn't need to be like this."

Sam ignored the phone. "Where are they?"

"Answer the phone."

Sam complied. "Yeah, I have him now…All secure."

"Why would you ever allow your daughter to work with you, knowing the danger of ops like this?" Nathan wanted Sam to know his story was blown. It was completely implausible. "You narcissistic fuck…putting your own flesh at such risk?"

Another strike. This time, Nathan's swollen eye began to deflate. The blow had created a deep cut below the eye lid.

"She isn't my daughter, you dumb shit."

"Of course she isn't your daughter." Nathan chuckled with disbelief. "Come on, do you really believe I fell for that story? This whole thing is one big setup. But your people underestimated me."

Nathan spit some blood out of his mouth.

"Fuck you!" Sam raged, grabbing his captive by the throat and squeezing. He let go before Nathan passed out.

"So it was a coded message I heard in the parking lot at the university?" Nathan turned his head, gasped for air, and allowed the blood flowing from his eye to drop to the floor. "She called you Daddy…Is that your call-sign?"

Sam refused to answer. "How did you hear the conversation?"

"I can hear every call she makes. Now I can hear every call you make."

"Where is your phone?" Sam slammed his hands against both of Nathan's ears hard enough to temporarily make him go deaf.

The chair Sam was sitting on fell to the floor as he stood. He rushed throughout the apartment, searching for the phone and Nathan's SAM device. He looked but found nothing.

Nathan opened and closed his jaw. The ringing in his ears was torturous.

"One of them's in Philly, another in Dallas, DC…Do you want me to go on?"

"What?" Sam stopped his search and looked in Nathan's direction.

"I told you…" Nathan leaned back with complete exhaustion. "The one I had was not the only one. You just fucked with the wrong guy."

At Nathan's remark, Sam dug back into his pocket and pulled out his phone. After pressing some numbers, he heard one ring and then the answer on the other end.

"You have the package?" the mysterious person on the other end asked.

"No." Sam walked back toward Nathan. "We have a problem."

"Bring him to me."

Sam cut Nathan's restraints. He pulled him to his feet. Through the nearby window, Sam could see the sun slowly beginning to rise. He needed to move with purpose, before New York City awakened.

Nathan didn't resist. He knew Sam was taking him into the lion's den, but this was exactly what Nathan desired. Taking a beating was nothing for him. He had experienced much worse throughout his career. But this time, he wasn't going to get beat by some foreign regime. No. This time, the beatings would come from members of his own country. They could beat him all they wanted, though. In the end, Nathan would win. He had plans…and his plans to take down the darkest within would eventually come to fruition.

EPISODE TWO

Despite being the city that never sleeps, New York City maintained a sense of deep quiet in its early morning hours. Nathan Belovich looked around his apartment and saw a disaster zone before his eyes. Steel handcuffs had been placed around his wrists, leaving his hands to dangle in front of his waist as he was shuffled out the door, wondering whether this would be the last he would ever see of the abode. He looked up toward the doorway where a painting of a war scene closely resembling one from a time he had spent in the mountainous regions of Afghanistan hung. He stopped in mid-pace and shook his head.

"What the hell was that?" Nathan's escort, Sam, stopped and grabbed his prisoner's collar from behind.

"The painting..." Nathan chuckled then stepped through the doorway. "Reminds me of a place I won't ever forget."

"Listen to me, and listen real good..." Sam placed his mouth next to Nathan's bloody ear. "Don't think I won't kill you."

"Kill me?" Amused, Nathan continued walking down the gloomy hallway. "No. You won't kill me."

"Let's just say that if you were a cat and had nine lives, you'd be living on life number nine." Sam nudged Nathan out of the building and onto a set of five concrete steps, which led to the street.

"I am way too valuable to your boss. With me dead, you will never know where to begin your search," Nathan declared as he stood by a black Suburban with limousine-tint windows.

"Get in." Sam pulled out his keys and unlocked the vehicle.

Nathan was trained in Kipling techniques. He knew to always observe his surroundings. Quickly identify the minutest details around him. Always retain what he saw for that one time when his situational awareness might become his lifesaver. What he saw on Sam's keys could be the thing to save him if the opportunity presented itself.

"So where are we headed anyway?" Nathan slid to a more comfortable position in the front passenger seat.

"You just get comfortable." Sam took one hand off the wheel and reached for his phone. "It's gonna be a long ride."

Nathan realized that Sam had placed himself in a predicament. Anyone with the slightest background in escorting prisoners knew never to handcuff anyone in the front. Never allow your prisoner to sit in the front seat, and always ensure they are seat-belted for added security. Then again, Sam wasn't wearing his own seatbelt, indicating he had some bad habits. Nathan believed Sam knew the rules but had underestimated his prisoner.

"Leaving the city now," Sam sighed into the phone. "I'm all secure."

The conversation was quick, and Nathan didn't have a chance to hear the voice on the other end of the line.

"Yeah, I have the package. Will conduct the exchange at the Water Gap."

The clock on the radio showed it was approaching six in the morning. More and more people were beginning to flood the streets. Nathan knew they were not hanging around New York for long, as they made a right-hand turn off Ninth Street, headed for the Lincoln Tunnel.

He did his best to analyze where he would be taken. He could think of only one Water Gap, so it was critical to solicit what he could to ensure his thinking was along the right lines.

"I love the Delaware Water Gap." Nathan lifted his hands toward his mouth to wipe some blood, which still trickled down his chin from the beating he had received earlier. He then fastened his own seatbelt. "Used to hike there. Nice mountains with great views."

"Shut up." Startled that Nathan was being so casual, Sam raised his voice.

Traffic leaving the city was minimal compared to the heavy volume of vehicles entering. Nathan realized the two were already on Interstate 80, making good timing as they headed westbound. That road would take him right to the Delaware Water Gap. The closer they got to Pennsylvania, the more desolate the surroundings became. As they neared the mountains of the Poconos, the need for Nathan to formulate a plan grew.

"So what's your real name anyway, Sam?" Nathan squinted as they passed a New Jersey state trooper running radar on the highway's median.

"You ask a lot of questions." Sam reached for a pair of sunglasses dangling from the rear-view mirror. "The more you talk, though, the more I think we crossed paths in our old lives."

"Let me guess…" Nathan perched upright and leaned his back against the vehicle's door. "JSOC? CAG? DEVGRU? OGA?"

"You got it all figured out, don't you?" Sam laughed at Nathan's flawless assessment.

Nathan focused on the road as they rumbled toward the merge where River Road and Old Mine Road became one. He knew this was the spot Interstate 80 crossed the Delaware River. A small island was located in the middle of the river, which indicated the water below him wasn't too deep, but that wasn't his major concern. It was do-or-die time. If he allowed the exchange, the prisoner transfer, to happen, the odds of having two escorts instead of just Sam were high. He realized letting himself be taken straight into the lion's den, or what he assumed was the base of this mysterious government entity holding him captive, was no longer the right move.

"Man, that's a low-flying chopper!" Nathan raised his handcuffed wrists toward Sam's window, hoping he would take his eyes off the road for just one second.

"What are you talking about?" Sam looked out the window. "I don't see anything."

Nathan grabbed the steering wheel and turned it toward him as far as it would go. The vehicle rocked hard toward the right, slamming into a guardrail. The Suburban wasn't the only thing to slam into a fixed object. Sam's head collided into the driver-side window, shattering glass, which scattered everywhere as the car became airborne, soaring over the bridge and into the river.

Nathan could only do so much other than cover his head in an attempt to protect it as the vehicle smashed into the river. Upon impact, water rushed into the half-sunken vehicle. Keeping his focus, Nathan reached for the keys in the ignition. He'd previously seen a handcuff key on the ring. He placed the keys in his mouth and then paused, looking at the body next to him. It was a body without any movement. It was a body devoid of sound. If Sam was dead, he could care less. Time was of the essence.

*Come on...*Nathan growled in pain as he pulled himself out of the broken front windshield.

Shit! Get his phone, Nathan. The voice inside his head served as a reminder of the actions he needed to take before fleeing the scene.

After one deep breath, he tucked his head into the water and lured his upper torso back into the vehicle. His hands floated in front of his body, protecting his head from any debris. His fingers ran across the dashboard and over the center console, feeling their way until he found what he was looking for.

Got it! Now get the hell out of here!

Nathan didn't bother unlocking the handcuffs yet. He could swim without the use of his arms, especially with the current running in the direction he wanted to go...south. He dolphin kicked as hard as he could until he reached the current that would swish him downstream. With his body moving in the direction he desired, Nathan rotated onto his back. A few hundred yards away from the bridge, he could see a few vehicles already stopped, and more were slowing down. He noticed only one bystander observing the wreckage in the water below. He was thankful the bystander wasn't looking at him.

Suck up the pain and keep going, Nathan said to himself as he tightened his muscles in an attempt to shake the cold from the mountain water rushing against his body.

The noise from Interstate 80 diminished as he continued downstream. He could see no small-town roads running alongside the river. Nathan realized the woods were getting thicker to his right and left. With his teeth beginning to grind, he knew it was critical to get out of the water and warm himself as best as possible.

He reached for the keys inside his mouth and fiddled with the one that could grant his hands the freedom they sought. Within a second or two, he was finally freed, allowing him to sidestroke to the Pennsylvania side of the river's bank. Reaching for a branch overhanging into the running water, Nathan pulled himself through heavy brush and onto dry land.

Pushups...do some pushups to get the heart rate going. Nathan continued to speak to himself, hoping the trick would keep him alive. Pain stung his left wrist as he pushed off against the ground.

God damn it!

Blood was draining out of his wrist, and it was paramount that he get some type of bandage around it to help slow the bleeding. During the crash, shattered glass must have become embedded between his wrist and the handcuff, causing a deep slice as he freed himself. Nathan had felt weak but believed it was the adrenaline surge fading. Now he knew the weakness came from a loss of blood.

Your shirt...Take off your shirt and make a bandage. Tie it tight. Make sure the knot is directly on the wound.

Nathan took off his shirt and once again realized the keys could be put to good use. Walking anywhere without a shirt during northeast Pennsylvania's fall months would be too ridiculous; it would draw too much attention. He needed the shirt, but he could still make the needed bandage. Using the keys as a knife, Nathan cut both sleeves off the garment and used them wisely.

There was enough foliage on the ground to provide for a decent hole-up site. With his wound temporarily treated, Nathan grabbed some nearby leaves and fluffed an ad hoc bed on the ground, which he hoped would allow him to keep enough body heat to stave off hypothermia. It was still early in the day, and the sun was strong enough to keep him warm, even with the forest canopy above.

His eyes became heavy. His body was shutting down. He lay silently on the leaves and allowed his fatigue to take over. Squirrels and birds along with other small wildlife chattered around him. He felt comforted by their sounds and used them to help bring him to sleep.

• • •

The team was loaded and ready. The sounds of wash coming from the helo's props added a sense of excitement for Nathan Belovich. Entering Al Qaeda's lair with hopes of taking out its leader in Tora Bora was a mission he had dreamed about for two years.

He would much rather operate with an Army SOF unit than with a bunch of SEALs, yet he understood his purpose and was well aware he had no control over those he would be attached to. Being joined with Red

Squadron was the least of his concerns. Surely an Air Force guy could handle a few Navy folks. Calling in a couple of air strikes would be nothing for the seasoned combat controller from the 24th STS. Poor intelligence, which lacked the precise number of enemy combatants, and some sketchy terrain served as his greatest concerns.

The team was twenty minutes into the flight. Another ten minutes or so and they would make contact with the first team, which had left only a moment before them. Soon, Nathan's team would be touching ground and engaging the enemy.

"We're aborting...!" The yell from the SEALs' master chief, who served as the team leader, resonated inside the humming chopper. For those too far away to hear, the leader's hand, running back and forth across his neck, signified the mission's termination.

"Chalk 1 should've grounded already." A SEAL, sitting near Nathan, raised his voice and directed it toward the team leader. "What do you mean we're aborting?"

"They were ambushed upon infil." The team leader placed his hand on his ear piece in an attempt to listen more closely to the action being relayed from the other chopper. "Never had the chance to offload the helo."

"Any casualties?" Ace, the team's medic, shouted.

The team leader failed to answer. He unbuckled his seatbelt, stood up from the red cargo seat, and rushed toward the flight deck to have a word with the pilots.

"One of our guys is on the ground..." Nathan overheard the master chief inform the pilots.

"A man on the ground?" Ace shouted, having heard too. "Thought you said they never offloaded."

"Fell out of the chopper." The chief turned from the flight deck and looked back at the team he was meant to lead into battle.

"What?" Jester, the designated automatic rifleman, placed his hand close to his ear, ensuring the team leader knew he needed the information repeated.

"Robby fell out." The master chief cupped his hands around his mouth, creating a make-shift loudspeaker. "Right when he unclipped, preparing to offload, an RPG fired at the bird. The pilot banked hard, and Robby fell about thirty feet to the ground."

Irv, the team's sniper, shook his head in disbelief. "We need to get him back!"

"The LZ is too hot." The pilot turned to the SEAL master chief. "We were ordered to return."

"You find a God damn place to land this thing! We don't leave men behind!"

"We have our orders, Master Chief." The pilot kept his hand on the throttle.

"I have a man down there, God damn it!" The team leader grabbed the pilot's shoulder. "I don't care if you drop us a mile out. We will hump it on foot."

The pilot shook his head for a second. "You don't get it. Chalk 1 aborted too. Took on heavy gunfire. The mission is scrapped."

"You tell that other helo pilot to follow us in." He pulled out a map and placed his finger on a ridge line located a hair more than a full mile away from the original landing zone.

"You go get your man. We'll provide as much cover as possible from above. We have just enough fuel to offload you and provide enough time for you to get your team secured on the ground. Then you're on your own, Chief."

"As soon as we ground, I'll call in for some air coverage," Nathan informed the chief, eager to get Robby back.

The team leader patted the pilot with appreciation and headed to the rear of the chopper. The rest of his team anxiously waited to hear any updates.

"Talk to us, boss." Ace, the medic, grabbed a nearby bottle of water and unscrewed the cap as the helo banked back toward the initial landing zone.

"All right, men…" The team leader sat on his seat and leaned forward so everyone could hear. "Robby is down. We're going in on a recovery mission. This bird is dropping us one click out, and we hump it in from there. Expect the worse. We leave no man behind!"

All nodded in agreement. This was no longer about Al Qaeda leadership. This was about the brotherhood and never leaving a man behind. After a few fist bumps, the team leader mandated all members ready their weapons.

"Lock and load, mother fuckers!" The chief pulled the charging handle back on his M4, ensuring a round was chambered. "One mike out!"

Nathan did as ordered with his weapon then sat silently. In the back of his head, he was rehearsing his communications to any air support they may need for this mission. It was his responsibility to call in air strikes and control all available air assets in the sky.

"Hey, bro…" Max, the stocky SEAL sitting across from Nathan, finished inserting a thirty-round magazine into his weapon. "Whatever you do, don't drop anything on us. Last time I was out, one of your guys dropped one danger close. Turned out it was more than just danger close.

Knocked me the fuck out, putting me out of the game for a couple of months due to the concussion."

Nathan looked at the concerned SEAL and the rest of the men waiting for infil. "This isn't my first rodeo. You cover me, and I will ensure the birds do what we need."

"All right, boys!" The master chief perched upright and, with a flip of his finger, released the single bar that had been locking his seatbelt. "No one goes to Valhalla without me!"

He exited the helo only feet prior to it touching ground. The rest of the men followed suit. Immediately, they moved into a three-sixty security formation, covering one another's sixes. Each prepared for the worst yet hoped for the best. Would their fallen comrade be recovered dead or alive? Only time would tell.

•••

The helo lifted, throwing dust and pebbles, and forcing the grounded team to cover their heads and protect themselves from the wash. As things settled, the team sat silently, conducting their SLLS checks. Stop, look, listen, and smell. The task was critical upon entering the unknown, to ensure no threat was nearby.

With a single hand encouraging them forward, the team moved out in a single file, headed eastbound on the rocky terrain of the mountainside. Fifteen minutes passed and the team's point man raised his fist. Those behind him froze in their tracks. A second or two passed and everyone took a knee.

"Talk to me, Jester." The master chief placed his hand on his throat, ensuring his whisper mic transmitted. "What do you see?"

"One tango. Twelve o'clock. One-fifty out." Jester raised his weapon and looked through his sites to see ahead of him more clearly. "Disregard last. Two tangos. It's a security team."

"Irv, take the high ground. Bring Nate with you."

"Roger that."

Irv, the team's sniper, tapped Nathan on the back. The two crouched and moved forward behind a boulder twenty paces above the other team members. It was the only decent cover and concealment available.

"Nate, get those air assets ready," Chief demanded and pulled out his monocular to observe. "There's a fucking army of tangos down there. Five hundred yards south-south east."

"You see our package?" the medic questioned after crawling closer to the team leader.

The master chief failed to respond. He needed to make sure the team nearby knew what they were up against.

"Viper 1, this is Viper 2." Chief attempted to make contact with the other team less than half a click to his west. No response. "Viper 1, come in."

"Go 'head, Viper 2." A familiar voice broke through from the other end of the transmission.

"I'm looking at about two hundred tangos, five hundred yards south-south east of my location." Chief placed his monocular back inside his kit. "All headed east on foot."

"Break. Break, break." Irv's voice interrupted the transmission. "Large convoy of vehicles parked three hundred yards east of tangos."

"Viper 2, this is Viper 1. What's the status of the blocking force?"

"82nd is three mikes out," Chief stated and looked down at his GPS.

"No one moves until they're in position."

Chief used his hand and arm to signal to his team. Everyone was to remain in place and maintain the appropriate security posture.

"Eyes on our package," Irv relayed into his radio and continued observing through his rifle's scope. "He's alive."

"Nate, I don't want them putting our boy inside one of those vehicles," Chief blurted through his whisper mic. He looked up to see whether Nathan had heard his instruction.

"Roger that," Nathan acknowledged and reached for the handheld attached to his SINCGARS radio. "I have Falcon 2 and 3 standing by."

"No more standing by. Make some shit happen."

Chief knew the incoming Chinooks loaded with his blocking force of 82nd Airborne would need a distraction to offload their platoon-sized element. Taking out the enemy's vehicles would offer enough mayhem for the Chinooks to temporarily land without any incident. And it would prevent the enemy from escaping into Pakistan.

Nathan didn't respond to Chief's last. He knew what he needed to do and began directing fire from the sky onto the enemies' staged vehicles. A moment passed and two A-10s flew above the vehicles, raining down thousands of 30 mm rounds until all of the enemy's vehicles were disabled.

"Let's get our package, boys." Chief shot to his feet and moved forward. The rest of his team followed his lead, excluding Irv and Nathan, who remained in place to provide cover fire if it was needed.

After rushing through a dead zone, the team established a hasty ambush position. It was easy for Irv to recognize their tactic, as it was something they rehearsed frequently. It was his duty to ensure no one could flank their position.

Below Chief spoke to the only man carrying a Squad Automatic Weapon. "Jester, get that SAW up."

An automatic volley of rounds freed themselves from Jester's weapon. Chief followed suit as he squeezed off a series of bursts from his M4. Max, loading his M203, squeezed the trigger and dropped several enemy targets after his M433 high-explosive dual-purpose grenade landed.

The ambush was a success but the battle was far from over. Then men began to bound forward, taking out as many enemy targets as they could.

"Sniper, ten o'clock. Four hundred meters," Nathan said to Irv. The target needed to be taken out before he got a shot off on Chief and his element.

"I got him," Irv acknowledged as he caught the sniper in his scope.

A single shot sounded from Irv's rifle. Before Nathan could blink, he watched the enemy sniper cave to the ground. Viper 1's team was in the fight too, taking out the enemy with hopes they would flee toward the blocking force, who would serve as the total annihilation factor.

"I'm hit!" Jester announced as his leg buckled and his body collapsed to the ground.

"Talk to me, Jester." Ace rushed toward his partner while continuing to unleash hell on any enemy he could.

"My leg!" Jester rolled onto his belly though he too continued providing cover fire, sucking up the pain that came with the wound. "My fucking leg! God damn it."

Ace sliced open Jester's pant leg to see the wound at mid-calf. "You'll be all right. Just hang in there."

"Bandage me up and get me back in the game, Doc!" Jester reached for ammo to reload the belt feed on his weapon. "Doc! Doc!"

Jester took his eyes off the enemy and turned to see why Ace had failed to acknowledge his request. It was a quick glance. He saw what he needed to. Ace lay motionless, his chest slightly rising and falling. A sign he was still breathing.

Chief looked over, his eyes wide. "Irv, my boys are pinned down here!" he relayed to his sniper.

"Stand by, Viper 1." Nathan checked the coordinates for the next fire run from his air assets, which would serve as a lifeline for Chief and his men.

Rounds pinged off the ground. Many were getting closer and closer to Chief's position. The enemy was locked on and determined to take out the SEAL element. Max did his best to drop as many targets as he could with his M203, but the enemy trudged forward.

"Get your guys in tight, Chief!" Nathan demanded. Any air support at this point could impact the very men he was supporting. "Ten seconds out."

Ten seconds later, as Chief pulled his last round and emptied his magazine, he looked up at the sky as if praying for some type of miracle, knowing his team was about to be completely taken out by the enemy.

"Get down!" he screamed at his men and blanketed his body over Ace's.

A series of explosions detonated over Chief's position.

Chief couldn't hear anything around him. His eyes were blurred but capable of seeing Jester roll onto his back and Max pull his weapon closer to his body.

"You all right, boss?" Max reached for Chief's arm. "Chief, talk to me!"

Chief smiled and then began to chuckle. His jaws opened and closed, accompanied by a quick shake of his head. He pulled his weapon closer and did his best to perch himself upright, to ensure any enemy that made it through the blast would be destroyed.

"Didn't you tell that fucker not to drop shit too close to us when we were on the helo?" Chief asked Max as he continued searching for any movement through the dust in front of him.

"I don't think he had any choice, boss." Max began to laugh. "Looks like you got the worst of that one. Better you than me this time. You all right?"

"Fuck you," Chief said with a smile, thankful to be alive.

"Will you two bastards get the hell off me?" Jester blurted from his prone position.

Neither Chief nor Max were on him. The two looked at Jester and realized they had lost one of their own. Ace was no longer breathing.

"God damn it." Chief stared at Ace's motionless body.

Max placed his fingers on Ace's neck, checking his vitals. "He's gone."

Things were quiet. Just a few pop shots erupting from nearby M4s. It was apparent the enemy was down and out."

"Viper 2, this is Viper 1. What's your status?"

"We're all secured," Chief announced over the radio. "We have one KIA and one WIA."

"Stay put. We're headed to you."

"Roger that." Chief moved to a more adequate position, maintaining a secured posture.

A single shot sounded in the distance. Nathan raised his head from behind the boulder, hoping to see where exactly it had come from. Irv beat him to the discovery.

"Shit." Irv was looking through his scope.

"Tell me that wasn't what I think it was." Nathan tried scanning the area.

"Chief," Irv announced over his radio.

"Go."

"They just took out our package." Irv quickly tucked the butt stock of his weapon into his cheek. "You have four tangos at your eleven o'clock. Headed toward the border."

"Viper 2, this is Viper 1. Stand down. Blocking force is in position."

Chief looked toward his left. Viper 1 and his element were approaching. A few of the men from the other team were conducting their battle damage assessments on the dead bodies of the enemy.

Chief quickly became merciless. The package he was after had been executed by the enemy, and he despised the thought that his own medic lay beside him, dead. "Come on!" He gestured to Max, and the two assisted one another to their feet. "Jester, we'll be right back. We ain't going far."

Walking around a crater caused by the recent bombing campaign, Chief observed several of the bodies. Some were missing limbs, blood protruded from the mouths and ears of others.

"You see these fuckers?" Chief asked Viper 1 as the two linked together and looked down toward the ground at one of the dead. "It's time we let their friends know who the fuck we are."

"Damn right." Viper 1 unsheathed a knife located on the side of his calf.

"There is a heritage among us who fight such savages." Chief spoke to one of the dead as though he could hear his words. He then grabbed the hair from the limp body's head. "We collect your fucking scalps!"

Just like the American Indians who once scalped the Europeans, Chief positioned the enemy on his stomach, pressed his feet hard against the enemy's shoulders, lifted the head toward the sky by grabbing the dead's hair close to its forehead, and began cutting the skin beneath. Once enough skin was lifted from the skull, Chief yanked the rest off with both hands until the scalp ripped away from the body.

Viper 1, with knife already in hand, began to do the same with a nearby corpse. The two were not alone, though. The entire SEAL platoon engaged in the war crime.

"Holy shit!" Nathan blurted as he maintained an overwatch position with Irv. "Tell me I'm seeing things."

"They get what they deserve," Irv replied as he continued looking through his sniper scope.

"Who?" Nathan squinted his eyes, perched on both knees, and looked again at the team of SEALs below. "Who gets what they deserve?"

"Wait a second." Irv took his eyes off his scope and turned to Nathan. "They executed Robby. Killed Ace. Have you never watched YouTube? Have you never seen them conduct their beheadings? Scalping these bastards is nothing compared to what they've done to some of our own."

"What good does this do?"

"It's a mark." Irv sat upright and pointed toward Nathan. "It's a mark so those who live never forget who the fuck we are. And guess what?"

Nathan stood in disbelief.

"You're part of us, whether you like it or not." Irv turned and repositioned himself in his overwatch position.

"This is bullshit." Nathan dropped back to the ground. There was nothing he could do at the moment. However, he discreetly turned on his helmet camera to tape what he was seeing.

"Exfil in twenty, Irv." Chief came through over the radio. "Get you and your boy down to the extraction point."

"Roger that," Irv replied and plucked himself to his feet.

A single crack resonated through the air. A bullet, one with Irv's name written on it, struck him smack in the face. The damage it caused would have made his own mother incapable of recognizing him. Startled, Nathan dropped to the ground again, taking cover.

"Man down. Man down," Nathan relayed over the net. "Sniper fire. Direction unknown. Irv is down."

"God damn it!" Chief blurted and rushed toward the closest cover he could find.

"I need exfil now!" Viper 1 stayed as low as possible, only feet from his master chief.

"Mongoose, get some eyes above, and blow that mother fucker to hell," Chief instructed and began peeking his head up to scan for the nearby sniper.

"Roger that, Viper 2." Nathan reached for the SINCGARS to contact any air assets above. The only assets nearby were the helos incoming for exfil.

"Viper 2, be advised, exfil re-routed to our location. Gunships providing cover fire as needed. No fix wings available at this time." Nathan grabbed his pack and threw Irv's limp body over his shoulder, running to the team's location below.

Upon arriving at Chief's location, Nathan gently laid Irv's body at the casualty collection point where Ace's body lay motionless. Nathan was briefly taken aback. He was more bothered, however, when he turned and saw Chief and the rest of the SEALs with blood covering their hands.

"What the fuck are you staring at?" Chief asked with rage when he saw Nathan's wide eyes. "Is there a fucking problem?"

"No, Master Chief. No problem. It's just…."

"Just what?" Chief walked closer toward Nathan.

"We lost two of our own." Nathan turned and pointed toward Irv and Ace's bodies.

Chief ever so slightly nodded. "We also lost our package."

"You mean Robby."

"First time you've seen teammates actually go down, huh?" Chief took a knee beside Ace and swept his hand over his eyes to close the lids.

Nathan simply nodded.

"So you got your cherry popped on this mission." Chief rose to his feet and walked toward Nathan without stopping. He passed the combat controller to collect his kit.

Nathan snapped out of his daze as he heard helicopters approaching. He turned and looked toward the sky. Two Chinooks began to land as one gunship hovered above.

"Let's saddle up, boys!" Chief shouted for all the men to hear and rushed toward the closest helicopter.

•••

The quiet in the woods was deafening enough to cause one of Nathan's eyes to open. The birds were silent, squirrels no longer stampeded through the leaves, even the subtle wind had died down. Nathan lay on the ground and scanned his surroundings.

Moments passed and the call of a wild turkey sounded in the near distance. But the lack of sound in the woods indicated to Nathan it wasn't a turkey he'd heard. No sooner, a man's voice materialized from close by.

"Hey, Pop, check this out!" a camouflaged hunter, toting a shotgun, shouted by the bed of the river.

"What do you got?" An older voice approached Nathan's direction.

"Fresh boot prints."

Nathan realized he was compromised. He knew if he continued hiding and was detected by the hunters, a confrontation could result. Hunters are territorial, and Nathan knew this well due to years of engaging in the trade as a young man.

He pulled some branches away from the hasty shelter and lifted his body off the leaves that had kept him warm.

The young hunter abruptly turned, pointing his weapon toward Nathan.

"Freeze!"

"I'm unarmed," Nathan replied and raised his hands in the air, cursing how loud he'd been.

"What the hell are you doing here?"

"Holy shit!" The gray-bearded hunter stumbled to the scene. "What the hell happened to you?"

"I got the shit kicked out of me." Nathan placed his hand close to his eye where he knew it had swelled black and blue. "Then they tried to abduct me."

"They?" the younger asked and began to walk closer to Nathan. "Who are they?"

"You wouldn't believe me if I told you." Nathan chuckled and crossed his arms in an attempt to bring warmth to his body's core.

"Try me."

"Son…" The elder interrupted and smirked. "You know he's not a threat. Look at him. Give 'im some space."

"How far are we from the bridge?" Nathan scanned his surroundings.

"About three miles." The younger's brows rose. "Wait a second. Were you in that vehicle?"

Nathan nodded, not withholding the truth.

"How the hell did you survive that crash?"

"I was recently told I was living on my ninth life." Nathan, with an obvious limp, walked closer to the two. "Guess whoever said that to me was wrong."

"Come on." The elder waved his hand. "We have a cabin not far from here."

"Sir, I appreciate it." Nathan shook his head slightly. "But I don't wish you or your family any inconvenience."

"Nonsense…" The elder shouldered his weapon. "You need some medical attention. At a minimum, you need to get cleaned up."

"Pop…" The younger frowned at his father in protest.

"You plan on trying to hurt us?" The elder's innocence was revealed.

"Sir, I don't plan on hurting anyone."

"Good." The elder turned back around and began escorting Nathan. "My family has a long history in the Marine Corps. I would hate to have to show a veteran what happens if they try anything stupid."

"How did you know I was a vet?" Nathan paused and stood, awaiting a response.

"Every time you address me, you start with the word *Sir*."

After a twenty-minute walk, Nathan and his escorts arrived at an old, 1960s log cabin. They were plentiful in northeast Pennsylvania, and this wasn't the first time Nathan had stepped foot in one. He spotted two vehicles out front and wondered why the two hunters would drive separately. There had to be more people around.

"Hey, hun, I'm gonna start the fire." The elder exclaimed as he breached the door and peeked inside. "We have one additional guest tonight for dinner."

"I'm Sean." The elder extended his hand toward Nathan. "This is my son, Jack."

"Pleased to meet both of you."

"So what branch were you in?" Jack sat on a large Pennsylvania bluestone near the fire pit.

"Don't hold it against me…" Nathan followed suit and sat on an old nearby stump. "Was Air Force."

"Air Force!" Sean blurted with a chuckle as he began to ignite the fire.

"Yup. I was one of those dumb Air Force guys, always assigned to an Army base."

"What were you?" Jack pulled out his pocket knife and began shaving wood off a dried stick to assist in creating tinder for his father's fire. "TACP?"

"Close." Nathan crossed his arms again, trying to shake the cold that saturated his body. "Combat control."

"No shit?" Jack took off the camouflaged sweatshirt he was wearing and tossed it to Nathan. "I watched one hell of an air strike several years ago that took out an entire contingent of Taliban. Rumor has it, it was coordinated by a JSOC team. It was a sight to see either way."

"Oh yeah?" Nathan slid the sweatshirt over his head. "What year were you there?"

"2003."

"Force Recon…" Nathan pointed at Jack's arm where a partial tattoo was displayed on the interior of his bicep.

"Yeah…" Jack looked down at the symbol of the skull, jump wings, and scuba bubble. "Was serving as one of their scout snipers at the time."

"Sounds like you and I were there during the same period."

Two women walked out of the house. One older than the other. They were carrying plastic Tupperware containers filled with food.

"Nathan…" Jack pointed toward the women. "This is my mother, Grace, and my wife, Carol."

Nathan stood and said, "It's a pleasure to meet you both."

The five sat around the campfire and ate a feast of burgers and hotdogs as the night fell and the fire's coals glowed red.

Soon Grace, Carol, and Sean were inside readying themselves for bed. Jack went to one of the vehicles to retrieve a sleeping bag for Nathan.

"You know…" Carol, who had returned outside, muttered quietly as she tossed a small branch into the pit. "When Jack came back home, he told me stories. Stories I couldn't believe. Stories he could never tell his father, as he fears his dad too wouldn't believe him."

"I don't care which war it was." Nathan took his eyes off Carol and stared up into the night. "If you were ever in combat, you saw something that will stick with you for a long time."

Carol nodded. "But the things he saw were done by our own. Horrible things. Things only savages would do to other human beings…"

Jack returned from the vehicle. In hand he had the sleeping bag tucked inside a stuff bag.

"Here…" Jack tossed the bag to Nathan. "Not a lot of room inside but at least this will keep you warm. Sorry the floor is all we have to offer."

"This will work." Nathan threw the bag lightly in the air and patted it with both hands. "Thank you."

Carol stood and walked toward the interior of the cabin. "See you guys in the morning."

"Good night, Carol," Nathan said.

"Be there in a minute, hun."

"So, Jack…" Nathan stood and placed his hands closer to the fire.

"I overheard Carol speaking to you." Jack too stood closer to the fire and warmed his hands. "If you're wondering, the terrible shit I saw was done by guys I supported. They were JSOC."

"I was with the 24th STS." Nathan looked across the fire pit and toward his veteran brother. "When I was in Afghanistan back in '03, I was attached to a SEAL unit. I saw things that have haunted me for a long time."

"Were you with the crew that lost one of their own?" Jack squatted in an attempt to warm the rest of his body. "You know…the team that had one of their guys fall out of the chopper?"

Nathan nodded.

"So you were part of that group?"

"I was attached to them." Nathan continued to stand. "I tried reporting it all as soon as we returned to Camp Vance. When I pulled out my helmet cam to show what I had captured on film, the commander started threatening me, and within a week, they pulled me back to Fort Bragg."

"So you pissed some SEALs off, and now they want you dead?"

"No, no…well, yes. But…" Nathan chuckled. "That's a part of the story I won't bore you with. Those who want me dead aren't SEALs. Let's just say, the incident in Afghanistan is only a part of it all, but now, without the footage, that incident will never surface in front of the public."

"What if you're not the only one who got video footage of that incident?"

"I hope I'm not." Nathan took a nearby shovel and threw some dirt on the fire, not wishing to leave the flames unattended prior to heading indoors. "But I don't believe anyone who has the footage has the balls to come forward."

"Do you?"

"Why not?" Nathan looked at Jack and placed the shovel against a tree. "What more do I have to lose?"

"I have the footage." Jack looked into the dying fire. "I make you a copy, promise me you get it in the public's eye."

"Why?" Nathan cocked his head. "Why would you want me to do this?"

"For closure." Jack turned and walked Nathan inside the cabin. "I have it in my house outside Philadelphia."

"So you were there?"

"I was operating a long-range recon mission." Jack stood in the doorway. "I was about a mile out. Heard everything unfold and started looking through my scope. It was a SEAL unit from Red Squadron."

"It was, but how did you know that?" Nathan asked. "I mean, how did you know they were from Red Squadron?"

"The patch." Jack pointed toward his own shoulder as if he were wearing the unit patch himself. "The Indian head and the two hatchets."

"You're good." Nathan smirked. "And you never reported what you saw that day?"

"Guess I wasn't as dumb as you." Jack patted Nathan on the shoulder and whispered so as not to wake his family, "Maybe I just feared what would happen to me, feared being taken out of the team."

"Yeah, well." Nathan turned and looked inside. "If you're not part of the solution…" he said quietly.

"You're part of the problem." Jack nodded in agreement. "This is why I'm willing to get you the tapes I have."

"I'm not going to be here in the morning," Nathan said. "I'll find a pen and paper and leave a note inside the pocket of this sweatshirt. It will have an address on it. A PO box. Send the tape to that address."

"You got it." Jack paused and turned to look at Nathan one last time before heading to bed. "You think you and I meeting today…You think it's just coincidence?"

"Crazier shit has happened in my life."

Jack cuddled up next to his wife in their room while his father and mother lay in the next room over. Nathan rested his sleeping bag on the floor near the cabin's entryway.

The tiny tucked-away log cabin was quiet and dark, which was comforting for a guy like Nathan Belovich. But as quickly as the night had blanketed the sky, the sun rose.

"He's gone," Carol whispered to Jack in the morning. "Just returned from the bathroom and saw he was gone."

"I'm sure we'll be seeing him again, someday."

EPISODE THREE

Mist sprayed high into the hull of the Boston Whaler as the boat breached three-foot waves upon exiting the inlet. The sun slowly began to crest the Atlantic's horizon, making the water sparkle. The cloud of early morning fog hovering over the island obscured the Wildwood Boardwalk.

"You comfortable driving this thing out to the reef?" Nathan Belovich braced his hand on a nearby rail close to the throttle as another wave made contact with the tiny vessel.

"Not one bit." Kellan Ponte, who was captaining the seventeen-foot single-engine, slowed the boat as another set of waves rolled toward them. He smiled. "Winter is approaching and stripers are hitting. We either go now or we miss out on the run."

"This is why I love you, man!" Nathan turned his ball cap backward in an attempt to prevent the wind from taking it off his head. "When it comes to striper fishing, nothing will stop you, will it?"

"I'm sensing the big bad tough-guy special operator is scared." Kellan threw the throttle forward as the last wave in the set passed.

"We're in a seventeen-footer…" Nathan turned and looked at his possessed brother-in-law. "I know it rides like a twenty-footer, but this is a bit concerning, don't ya think?"

"It'll calm the closer we get to the reef." Kellan continued to breach each wave that approached, often getting air between the hull and the fifty-two-degree ocean water.

The boat slowed as Kellan put it in position for the drift over the Cape May Reef. Nathan grabbed three rods and threw on the fresh clams, which would be used as bait. A few boats floated nearby. Nathan dropped the lines, and within seconds, he felt action bouncing off the wreckage of New Jersey's largest artificial reef.

Kellan chuckled out loud as he looked down at his cell phone. "It's gonna be a great day for fishing!"

"Let me guess…" Nathan grabbed one of the poles and placed it in a holder on the side of the boat. "Wife texted you, saw the weather report, and made some remark about how we're crazy for being out here right now."

"Not quite."

"Well, what's so funny then?"

"Just looked at my Sea Tow app." Kellan showed Nathan the phone. "Looks like it's only going to get rougher as the day goes on."

"Says we should expect up to five-foot waves." Nathan removed his sunglasses to get a better look. "Do you realize what a bitch it's going to be getting this thing back into the dock?"

"We'll just take it nice and slow."

The pole Nathan placed in the holder tugged downward and popped back up. The reef below had a tendency to make the rods bounce, but not that hard. The commotion was a striper taking a hit at the bait.

"Get ready to hook that baby!" Kellan directed Nathan as he rushed toward the boat's console. "The fish finder is showing we have a whole bunch below us."

Nathan placed the rod in his hand into one of the spare holders on the side of the boat and grabbed the one wriggling about. "I got 'im!"

"Keep it tight!" Kellan reached for the net then shouted with excitement, "Fish on, baby!"

Nathan lowered the tip of the pole and reeled the line, trying to keep everything as tight as possible. He firmly lifted the pole upright again. The fish was fighting and continued to take the line out to sea in desperation.

"You're on your own, brother!" Kellan dropped the net and reached for another pole, which had begun to dance. "I'm hooked too! Whoo-hoo!"

"Now we're fishing!" Nathan blurted as he threw his fingers into the gill of the thirty-plus-inch striped bass.

"Nate, grab the third pole!" Kellan pointed with one hand as he continued to reel. "Looks like we got another one hitting."

"Holy shit!" Nathan took a deep breath and rushed toward the remaining pole. "Got 'im!"

With one keeper in the boat and two shorts released, adrenaline surged through both fishermen. Nathan and Kellan didn't wait to celebrate. Both men took more fresh clams out of their shells and slipped the balls of slime onto the hooks in hopes of catching the stripers nearby.

More than a half-hour passed without another bite.

"You notice what just happened?" Nathan asked as he looked out onto the ocean's horizon.

"Yeah!" Kellan grinned. "We just had three fish on at the same time!"

"No." Nathan continued to scan his surroundings. "I'm not talking about that."

"Well, what then?"

"It's calm."

"I told you that once we got out here things would calm a bit."

"Look around us." Nathan dropped his sunglasses onto the bridge of his nose. "Where did the boats go? There were boats out here when we arrived. Where did they all go?"

"You're paranoid." Kellan slightly tugged his rod. "A lot of these guys can only go out for an hour or two, and then they need to head in. It's a work day. Not everyone can take a full day off with this economy."

"No." Nathan protested and shook his head. "Something isn't right. We're the only ones out here."

"Well, I ain't leaving." Kellan sat on the ledge of the stern, holding one of the rods. "The sun is out, almost no breeze at all. The drift is perfect. Water temp is optimal…No way…We aren't going anywhere."

"Is your radio on?" Nathan placed his rod down and stepped toward the boat's console. "Your radio isn't working."

"It's been giving me a hard time lately." Kellan looked at his brother-in-law. "It works when it wants to. I was planning on getting it checked next week when I dry-dock the boat for the season."

"So, Mr. Brilliance," Nathan stood in disbelief, "if something happens and we need the radio, what's your plan? How do you expect to communicate with anyone?"

"Listen, I have been out here hundreds of times with no issues. I know the radio goes on and off when it wants. We're fine." Kellan opened a door below the steering column. "I have flares, a signaling mirror, and a handheld. Oh yeah, and I have my Sea Tow app too, which works perfectly…I know, I have used their service before."

"You really are nuts." Nathan shook his head.

"Fish on!" Kellan shouted as a fish took the bait.

"So this is how you're successful at catching these things?" Nathan rushed to grab the net. "I give you a hard time for being a stupid boat owner, and you begin catching all the fish?"

Kellan could only laugh as he began to reel.

"It'll be close." Kellan looked through the water's surface to see the fish. "I don't think that's twenty-eight inches."

"Bring it in, and we'll measure." Nathan dipped the net into the water and scooped the fish into the boat.

"Toss it back." Kellan looked down at the flopping sea creature, already seeing that it failed to meet New Jersey's mandated length. "It's an inch or so short."

•••

The drift through the reef was over. The men pulled the rods into the boat, and Kellan drove the vessel southbound for another pass. Despite the Sea Tow app's warning, the environment appeared perfect as the mid-morning sun beamed down.

"Hey, man." Kellan reached for a pole. "It's just you and me right now…"

"What's on your mind?" Nathan dropped a line into the water.

"What really happened to your face?" Kellan looked at his brother-in-law. "I know you didn't get into some bar fight."

"I'm in some deep shit, buddy." Nathan ran his finger under his blackened eye. "And to be honest, I don't know how I'm getting out of this one."

"Government shit?"

Nathan smirked. "You can say that."

"You know, I never knew exactly what you did or who you worked for. Yeah, I knew you were former military…Air Force…but after your military career, I never asked questions. But let me ask you something now."

"Send it."

"When my sister died…"

"Leah's death had nothing to do with anything I am involved in." Nathan placed the rod in its holder and turned to look at his brother-in-law. "She was at the wrong place at the wrong time. It was a robbery gone wrong. You know that."

"And you never thought for one second it could have been a setup?"

"Not until now."

"Nathan, look at your face." Kellan flung his finger at Nathan. "Who the fuck is after you? Tell me. I'm the only guy you've ever trusted. You tell me that all the time. Just tell me what the fuck is going on."

"When I was on active duty, I was assigned to JSOC." Nathan reached for the side of the boat as it rocked from a small wave. "We did things no one could ever imagine. Some of the guys did things I couldn't have imagined. I'm talking about serious war crimes."

"And they are after you…why?"

"Because they fear I am going to blow the whistle on them. I know too much about their past and what they're doing today: from war crimes to technological advancements they're abusing…and a whole lot more."

"Are you…planning to blow the whistle on them?"

Nathan didn't answer but rather provided more concerning information.

"When I left active duty, I started working for a dark entity...one that makes the CIA look like chumps...one that doesn't really exist...one that is managed by some of the country's most powerful. Our funds came directly from private entities, mostly the big banking industries...all former SOF operators and clandestine types...Our mission was to turn nations upside down."

"Wait a second." Kellan braced himself against the boat. "You're telling me some government organization that isn't the CIA does things like that?"

"Nope." Nathan bent his knees in an attempt to keep his balance as the boat began to rock more violently. "This is all private. Guys who are no longer part of the government simply getting a paycheck from the big wigs on Wall Street."

"But the last I heard you were doing some adjunct work at a university or something."

"I was placed in that position to monitor some things, to recruit, influence, manipulate." Nathan reeled up the line to check the bait. "They have guys in virtually every major institution here in the States. They also have guys who've infiltrated international organizations and foreign governments."

"So why the hell are these guys after you?"

"I guess you could say I found my conscience."

Kellan's cell began to vibrate. He reached into his pocket and looked on the screen to find a weather alert. A major storm was moving in.

"We need to get the hell out of here." Kellan placed the phone back in his pocket and started to reel up the lines. "Bad storm approaching."

"You're ready to accept some common sense." Nathan laughed at the timeliness of the alert, which came once Kellan had captured his quota of fish.

"I'm getting hungry anyway." Kellan moved himself behind the wheel and pushed the throttle forward. "Let's get back and go to the Dog Tooth for a bite…I'm buying."

"Now that sounds like a plan."

•••

One of very few watering holes open all year round in Wildwood, NJ, also happened to serve some of the best bar food. The Dog Tooth was one of Nathan's favorite hot spots, not just for the food and booze, but because of the woman who worked behind the bar—Rene Jaspers.

"What the…" Rene, shocked to see Kellan and Nathan walk in, dropped the rag in her hand atop the old wooden bar. "Oh my God!"

"Nice to see ya again." Nathan smiled and leaned forward to kiss Rene on the cheek.

"Can I get whatever IPA you have on draft?" Kellan asked with discomfort, knowing it was Rene's bed Nathan had found comfort in after his sister was killed. "Whatever you have on draft will work."

Without hesitation, Rene filled a pint and handed it to Kellan then said, "It's been a while, Nate. You still drinking Scotch?"

"I think I'll just have what he's drinking for now." Nathan looked over to his brother-in-law and gave him a mild nudge with a smile.

"You look great, except for that shiner you're sporting." Rene handed Nathan a brew.

"Yeah…" Nathan rubbed his finger near his eye. "You're looking good yourself."

"Thanks. Listen, I need to run out for a while," Rene said, showing her dimples as she smiled. "I have an appointment I need to be at in ten minutes. Grover is going to cover for me while I'm away. Don't leave until I come back."

"We're just eating then heading back to the house." Kellan took a swig. "I'm working as the FTO tonight."

"Field training officer?" Nathan laughed. "I thought the days of you taking rookies out on the road were over."

"Just helping out one of my guys who needs the night off," Kellan replied and cockily looked at the female bartender. "So yes, Rene, I am eating and running."

Rene grabbed her purse and keys from under the bar and rushed toward the door, stopping right before she exited the premise. "I don't even know why I try being nice to you anymore. By the way, if you're working tonight, do you think you should be drinking? You'll be carrying after all. A bit hypocritical, I think."

"You know, she is right." Nathan looked at the stuffed marlin on the wall across from them. "You don't like Rene. But she isn't dumb. Rene and I hooked up more than a year after Leah died. You know just as well as I do that she's a good woman."

"I know…"

"She is looking good these days…You have to admit it."

"Rene was always hot, Nate."

"You know if she's with anyone?"

"No clue." Kellan finished off his drink and signaled to Grover for a refill. "Question for you, Nate."

"What's up?"

"That shit you were talking about when we were out earlier today on the boat…" Kellan reached for his newly filled glass. "What's next? I mean, what are these not-so-government operators going to do next?"

"Who knows." Nathan placed his hand on his temple. "I heard a rumor that they were going to do something right outside the Panama Canal."

"The Canal?" Kellan perked upright.

"Remember that huge cargo ship we saw out on the horizon earlier today?"

"Yeah?"

"An Iranian company transits the Canal pretty regularly." Nathan glanced passively throughout the bar to see if anyone was nearby. "The ship is loaded with Iranian oil."

"Those guys aren't going to try to blow up the ship while it's in the Canal, are they?"

"They aren't that stupid." Nathan chuckled and sipped the fuzzy brown liquid in his glass. "No. They will wait for it to leave the Canal, which serves as a choke point. From there, they will follow it back out into international waters. It's then that they'll hijack the vessel."

"Why hijack the vessel?"

"Some court in the US found Iran guilty of atrocities that resulted in the deaths of some US persons. All Iranian terror related. Shit went as far back as the incident in '83 where a couple hundred US Marines were killed in Beirut."

"I read something about the US seizing Iranian assets here in the States for similar reasons."

"Freezing an asset doesn't do anything for the family members." Nathan reached over the bar and grabbed a menu. "The guys I was associated with believe the only way to help the families of the victims is to help alleviate some of their struggles with financial compensation."

"Yeah, but how will hijacking a cargo ship help do that?" Kellan opened the menu Nathan had grabbed.

"If it's filled with oil, problem solved, right?"

"I don't know if I'm following all the way." Kellan dropped the menu on the bar next to his half-empty glass. "Hey, Grover, can I get one of those grouper sandwiches?"

"Make that two, please." Nathan raised his finger, ensuring Grover knew to double the order. "I told you that these guys are well connected to some heavy hitters in Wall Street."

"So?"

"Those heavy hitters know precisely where to go to turn commodities into cash." Nathan scooted himself off the stool and stood near his brother-in-law, taking a deep stretch. "These guys have the means to move a vessel just outside a South American port, offload the commodity, and turn it into hard cash."

"No way!"

"They have done it with diamonds and other high-value commodities, and they're doing it with oil today." Nathan chuckled, thinking about how easy the operations were to conduct. "When you have the right system in place, with the right people backing you, and you target entities most Americans despise, it's not difficult to pull off. How do you think they've been funding themselves for so long?"

"So these guys are taking a cut out of everything?"

"Trust me, if they were ever caught doing what they're doing, most Americans would look at them as patriots." Nathan wiped some of the slaw away from his lips as he tasted the recently-arrived order. "But if they looked more closely, they'd find they're just as corrupt and evil as the bad guys."

"Are you really going to blow the whistle on them? They'll kill you, won't they?"

"So others may live." Nathan sipped what was left of his brew. "That's one of the mottos."

"So who are these others you're speaking about?"

"People the military has forced into ideological wars, which more often than not, American entities actually started or at least helped fuel."

Once the men were well into their sandwiches, the bells on the door to the bar clanked overhead. In came a wavy-blond-haired, blue-eyed woman Nathan knew too well. Her skin-tight jeans and knee-high boots, along with a sky-blue button down, were the sexiest things Nathan had seen in a while.

"You ready to get out of here?" Kellan asked as he threw down a pair of twenty-dollar bills.

"I think I'm going to stick around for a while."

"Should I assume I won't see you for several months?" Kellan stood. "I mean, I know how you roll. You pop in, and just as quickly, you disappear."

"I guess only time will tell."

●●●

The newly constructed townhouse only a block away from the George Redding Bridge, off Route 47, didn't resemble any traditional New

Jersey shore home. But for Rene, it was home all the same. The first place she had actually owned.

"Want a drink?" Rene asked as Nathan looked through the sliding glass door in the upstairs living room.

"You have a great view of the bay here." He looked around the room at the décor, noticing the picture near the television. "Your new squeeze?"

"That's Gary." With a glass of water in hand, Rene walked toward Nathan. "It's only been about six months."

"Coast Guard?" Nathan noticed the uniform in the picture.

"Rescue swimmer." Rene turned Nathan away from the photo. "It's nothing serious."

"Does he know that?"

Rene responded by grabbing the back of Nathan's head and forcing her tongue into his mouth. Nathan was quick to protest, pushing himself away. His hands gripped Rene's slender waist and he looked into her eyes, seeing her intensity.

"Don't you do this to me, Nathan Belovich," Rene whispered as her head drooped toward the floor. "I was willing to put my life on hold for you. Please, don't make me wait any longer."

"I told you long ago that I don't deserve you." Nathan placed a hand on the back of Rene's head, pulling it into his chest. "What happened? What happened to the back of your head? You have a bump."

"It's nothing." Rene backed away.

"Bullshit."

Rene took several steps backward, closer to a nearby sofa. After a few moments, her fingers unbuttoned the blouse she was wearing, allowing it to slowly fall off her shoulders and expose her bare torso and a navy-blue bra.

Nathan stood in shock. "Did he do this to you?"

A simple nod. Her hands crossed over her breasts, each hand holding onto her biceps, which displayed bruises.

"Where is he?" Nathan remained calm and walked toward Rene. "Tell me where he is."

"He won't return to Cape May for another day or two." A teardrop slowly trickled from Rene's left eye. "He's stationed there. He scares me, Nathan."

"Is that why you won't leave him?"

Another nod. "If you hurt him, it will only make things worse."

"Where is he right now?" Nathan asked calmly, a look of curiosity on his face.

"Florida." Rene reached down to pick up her blouse. "At least that's what I was told. He said he was going on some training exercise."

"Why didn't you talk with Kellan?" Nathan sat on the sofa and reached for Rene's hand. "You know he could have stopped this."

"I was scared to get the cops involved."

"Kellan is smart. He would have known how to handle this. He's been with the state police long enough to know." Nathan rested Rene's head on his lap. "Did you really think Kellan wouldn't have helped you? Shit, he lives less than a block away from here."

"Unless you're in this type of situation, you will never understand, Nate."

Nathan was silent, then, "I promise he will never touch you again."

Rene lifted her head and kissed Nathan. This time, he did not protest as she crawled on top of his lap. Her fingers ran through his short brown hair. Her lips moved to the side of his neck.

Nathan was quick to maneuver Rene off him. "He's home."

"What are you talking about?"

"The door downstairs…" Nathan turned his head to listen for movement. "The door just closed."

"Yeah, he's home, mother fucker!" A strange voice emanated from the stairwell. "You're dead, bitch!"

Filled with fright, Rene attempted to dress herself as quickly as possible, all the while backing into a corner. Nathan walked toward the center of the room, waiting to meet the man who had put his hands on Rene.

"I suggest you get the fuck out of here," the abuser said as his eyes grew red. "Now!"

"If I leave, she's coming with me." Nathan said calmly and stood his ground. He waved toward Rene. "C'mon. We're leaving."

"You have one second, mother fucker." Gary strode closer to Nathan. "And she isn't going anywhere."

Rene hurried to the coffee table, reached for her phone, and pressed a series of numbers.

"Oh no you don't!" Gary rushed toward her.

Nathan extended one arm and placed his hand on the attacker's forehead, tilting it backward. With his opposite hand, he pushed onto Gary's lower spine, quickly bringing the assailant to the ground.

"You're not touching her," Nathan stated in a collected voice while side-stepping the fallen body. He waited for Rene to move toward the stairs and out of the house. "Come on, Rene."

Rene didn't follow but rather spoke into the phone. "Yes, please, I need you to come to 4 Mediterranean Ave."

"Rene, we need to go outside and wait for the cops there." Nathan reached for the blond-haired woman, who stood only feet away from her nightmare. "Let's go."

"You're not going anywhere." Gary stood.

"Fuck you, Gary!" Rene screamed with panic.

"No. Fuck you, whore." He reached into the side of his waist then pointed his concealed pistol. "You fucked with the wrong guy."

"It doesn't have to be like this." Nathan let go of Rene's hand and neared Gary, who took a step closer to Nathan. It was a mistake and Nathan now knew the type of amateur he was dealing with. The closer Gary moved, the easier he would be to disarm.

"Head shot? Center mass?" Nathan asked as he prepared his next move. "What will it be, Gary? Two to the chest and one to the head? Is that what you were taught?"

Gary smirked and began to move his pistol across the room until it was aimed at Nathan's heart. Prior to the movement's end, Nathan bladed his body and stepped inward, closing the distance. One hand pushed Gary's gun-hand to the outside of both their bodies, while Nathan's other hand reached up under the slide to secure the weapon.

Nathan torqued the gun, turning it 180 degrees until the barrel faced Gary's torso. Gary's finger was trapped in the trigger guard. The twisting forced his finger to press the trigger. As Gary lurched backward, Nathan stripped the weapon free and delivered two more shots.

"Oh my…" Rene placed her hand over her mouth and looked at Nathan. "He's…"

"Dead."

•••

Sirens approached from the distance. The closer they got, the more tense the situation became. Three vehicles skidded in front of the house, and a loud bang resonated against the door.

"It's the police. Open the door!"

Rene ran down the stairs to the front of the house. Her hand twisted the doorknob, allowing the law enforcement officers entry. They rushed up the flight of stairs to the sight of Nathan standing with gun in hand.

"Drop the weapon!" one of the cops shouted, his gun drawn.

Nathan placed the pistol on the ground, raised his hands in the air, and backed away.

"Viper 2 to station." The police officer spoke into his radio. "Be advised, we have one down. I need medical."

Nathan recognized the voice. He recognized the well-built physique and all the facial features. More alarmingly, he recognized the call-sign.

"Viper 2?" Nathan muttered with his hands still overhead. "Former US Navy SEAL? A master chief?"

"You're in a lot of trouble." The patrolman aimed his weapon. "Get on the ground!"

"He didn't do anything!" Rene shouted and rushed between the cop and Nathan. "He took the gun away. The gun belongs to Gary. Nathan saved my life."

"On the ground!" the cop screamed.

"Rene, this is Officer Victor O'Day." Nathan slowly placed one knee on the ground. "He is a former master chief Navy SEAL."

"Shut your mouth!" The cop aimed his weapon at Nathan's head.

"You know him?" Rene looked at Nathan, panicked.

"He has been looking for me for some time now." Nathan rose back to his feet, refusing to lie on the ground. "If you're going to kill me, Chief, I won't allow you to do it while I'm submitting."

"I have no clue what you're talking about." The cop stood firm as his two counterparts moved across the room in defensive positions. "I was never a SEAL."

"You don't remember me, Chief?" Nathan snickered. "I was your JTAC, your combat controller. I was the one who called in that air strike that saved you and half your team several years ago in Afghanistan."

"Looks like you need some help, son." The cop placed his hand forward, suggesting Nathan go to the ground. "I need you to lie on the ground for your own safety. I need to make sure you have no weapons on you."

"No, Chief." Nathan indiscreetly eased himself closer to the gun he had previously used. "You've been looking for me. You know I have details of what you did to those Afghans. What you did to their dead bodies. What you and your team of rogue operators are up to today. You know I know everything."

"Nathan…" Rene pleaded. "Nathan, what are you talking about?"

"OK, I've had enough of this." The cop looked at his two partners standing by. "Get her out of the way. I want her secured."

Two cops reached for Rene and violently threw her to the ground. One placed the back of his knee on her lower spine while the other forced her hands behind her back.

"Nathan!" A familiar voice boomed from the downstairs doorway.

"Don't move!" The main police officer whipped around and pointed his weapon at the incoming person.

"I'm a cop!" Kellan rushed up the stairs, flashing his badge. "State police."

"Kellan, remember what I told you about earlier today?" Nathan turned and looked at his brother-in-law. "Remember everything I mentioned while we were on the boat?"

"Son, you need to remain quiet!" The cop pointed his weapon back at Nathan.

"Nathan, do as you're told," Kellan demanded and continued to move toward the center of the room. "Everything is going to be all right."

"No, Kellan. Everything isn't going to be all right."

"Nathan, you have to trust me." His brother-in-law reached his hand out to Nathan, virtually begging him to listen.

"Kellan, this is Viper 2. I served with him in Afghanistan. I told you about that ordeal. He's part of the system I spoke to you about today."

Kellan looked as if he were in disbelief. "Please, just do as you're told."

"I told you, brother. They want me dead."

Kellan began to position himself between the cop and his brother-in-law. "We will help you, brother. I promise. Please, just do what you're told. Let me take care of you."

"He is going to kill me."

"No one is going to kill anyone." Kellan reached for his handcuffs. "Let me get you out of here. I will personally transport you."

Nathan saw a glimmer in Viper 2's eye. The cop's gun was startling to Nathan as it continued to point in his direction.

"Kellan." Nathan slid ever so slightly closer to the weapon on the ground. "Don't forget my story."

He rushed for the gun he'd used on Rene's abuser. His hand secured it while his body rolled sideways, just passing the coffee table nearby. He was quick to pop himself up to one knee and obtain the proper alignment he needed to take out his target.

A shot echoed in the room followed by a deafening silence.

EPISODE FOUR

"How are you feeling?" a soft and calming female voice asked.

"How did I do?" Nathan Belovich opened his eyes and looked at the blond-haired woman standing beside where he lay.

"You did fine," she said. "You did just fine."

"I'm exhausted." His face appeared confused. "I'm soaked with sweat."

"You were having nightmares."

"I know."

"You know?" The female doctor looked confused this time.

"I remember everything."

"Everything?" she asked.

He nodded and placed his head back on the pillow.

"Nathan, I'll be right back." She gently placed her hand on his chest. "Can I get you anything?"

"Doc…"

"You can call me Rene."

"Rene…can you get me some water?"

After a subtle smile, Rene turned and started to leave the room. Nathan lay with his eyes wide, staring at the light hanging from the ceiling.

Rene?

"Wait." He slid himself upright. "Where am I?"

She turned in the doorway and strode back to her patient. "I thought you remembered everything."

"I'm confused." He placed his hands over his face.

"You remember everything you dreamt but you don't know where you are or why?" Rene pulled out a pen and began taking notes on a notepad previously tucked inside a pocket of the white doctor's coat she wore.

"I'm in a hospital." He closed his eyes tightly, revealing crow's feet as he dug deep into his memory. As his fingers touched his forehead, he violently threw them onto his chest with panic. "The last thing I remember was training at Camp Dawson. Was I shot?"

"No, Nathan." Rene placed her hand on his forehead in an attempt to comfort him. "You weren't shot. You had a nightmare. In it, you dreamt you were shot by the police. You left West Virginia—Camp Dawson—weeks ago after you completed the training."

"I don't understand," Nathan said calmly while trying to find answers in his mind. "How do you know what I was dreaming about?"

"If you give me a minute, I will bring in my boss, and together, we will explain everything to you…why you are here, what you went through, and so forth."

"I'm not safe here," he whispered as he closed his eyes. "They are going to kill me. You were there. We were together. Wait. You're my girlfriend? It's coming back to me."

"No one is trying to kill you, Nathan." Rene blushed. "Your dream was a bit sexual, though, and I was a bit embarrassed that you included me in it."

"How do you know all of this?" Nathan cocked his head in question. "How do you know what I was dreaming about?"

"I was monitoring your dreams."

"Rene…" Nathan reached for the doctor's hand. "Promise me I will be OK."

Rene smiled. "Just give me a second and things will become much clearer for you."

Before Rene could leave the room, a well-built man in his early fifties walked in. He was dressed in a suit and held a briefcase. His shoes clicked as he walked through the room. His face was memorable.

"I know you." Nathan glared past Rene, observing the man's slicked-back ponytail.

"Of course you do." He sat in a nearby chair. "I was your course instructor while you were in Dawson."

"No." Nathan slid back in the bed. "You go by Sam. You tried to kidnap me. You died in the accident. The car…I swerved the vehicle into the guardrail. We went over the bridge and into the river. You died."

"Nathan, this is Sexton Colver. He is the man who has been training you," Rene explained. "After you left the military, you were recruited to become one of America's most highly trained operators. You went through a rigorous training venue in West Virginia. Then you came here for an extended period for neurological and biological tests."

"Son, you did everything we asked of you." Sexton smiled. "Out of the ten candidates, you were the only one to actually make it."

Nathan lay silently. He turned his head slightly away from Sexton. He began to recall the things they were saying.

"Nathan, the training you went through was unlike anything anyone could imagine." Sexton pulled out his briefcase, which contained photos of Nathan training in West Virginia. "You were tested to your physical and mental limits."

"The physical tests were conducted at Camp Dawson." Rene stood by her patient's side. "The mental, neurological, and biological portions you completed here. You are at the Aberdeen Proving Ground."

"Son, you're going to stay here for several more days. We are going to continuously evaluate you, see how you're coping with everything. As I said, you did an outstanding job."

"Stay here?" Nathan's eyes widened. "In this hospital?"

"No," Rene interjected. "Later this afternoon, I will walk with you to a different area. It's really nice. We know you'll like it. You'll have your own temporary home with your own bedroom, kitchen, and living room—everything you need. You will be able to go to the pool, the gym. You will pretty much be free to do what you want."

"You just won't be able to leave the base, Nathan." Sexton reached into his pocket, pulling out a small syringe. "For your own safety, I need to know where you are at all times."

"What's in it?" Nathan looked at the object in Sexton's hand, already forming a guess. "What's in the syringe?"

"This has a tracking device in it." Rene reached for Nathan's wrist as Sexton handed her the syringe. "The tracking device will be positioned opposite your palm, on the top of your hand. It won't hurt once it's in place, and you will forget it's even there."

"Is that similar to what they put in dogs?" Nathan looked down as Rene positioned the needle between the two veins that bulged at the top of his hand. The needle penetrated and she pushed the tracking device forward, deep under the skin.

"Finished," she said.

"Now what?" Nathan asked and continued to stare at his hand.

"Now we give you some space." Sexton placed the photos back in his briefcase. "You need some time, Nathan, to recover from everything you went through. And we are going to ensure you get the time you need. You're one of America's most valuable assets, son."

"I will escort you to your quarters after lunch," Rene said and looked down at her watch. "It should be here soon."

"Nathan…" Sexton uttered as he eased away from his trainee. He was dressed well, but his clothes weren't pretentious. He gave off a respectable air. "If you need anything, Rene will take care of you. She knows how to get a hold of me. I will see you in about a week or so." He paused. "Everything you went through is incredibly unique and highly classified. While I am away, understand that you cannot speak with anyone about anything that happened, excluding Rene."

"My own designated nurse, huh?" Nathan snickered. "What happens when people start asking me questions? What do I say?"

"You were taught tradecraft." Sexton stood by the door. "You will find that things will come naturally to you. You will eventually understand how good you really are. And, you may even impress yourself as much as you impressed us."

"Is this for real?" Nathan asked Rene as Sexton walked out of the room.

She nodded with a smile.

•••

The home wrapped in red brick was old yet inviting. Nathan walked through the door and saw a warm living quarter meant for high-ranking generals. Rene helped him through the house and showed him everything inside.

"It's beautiful," Nathan blurted and glanced through the fully furnished house.

"Are you tired?" Rene asked and placed her hand on the back of Nathan's shoulder. "Can I get you anything?"

"Answers."

"I figured you would have plenty of questions." Rene smiled and sat on a nearby sofa.

"Not there." Nathan was startled, remembering his dream from earlier. "Can you sit on the rocking chair?"

"I'm so sorry, Nathan." Rene complied. "I forgot."

"How do you know these things? How do you know what I dreamt about?"

"We have abilities to not only monitor but also control people's dreams." Rene sat on the oak rocking chair and placed her hands on top of her thighs. "We have the most advanced medical testing facilities in the world."

"But why? Why would you want to monitor my dreams?" Nathan sat on the sofa Rene had previously claimed. "I just don't understand."

"Your dreams come from your subconscious state." Rene leaned forward. "In the world you have entered or, rather, will enter, you will be tasked to perform unique operations."

"Go on."

"The operations you will conduct may appear immoral to many, controversial to most—these are not operations just anyone can perform."

Rene stood and walked toward a nearby television. "With so many secrets being leaked these days, we need to ensure those who conduct the types of operations you will perform are...well...leakproof."

"And through studying my subconscious behaviors, you determined whether or not I'm safe?" Nathan interlaced his fingers and tilted his head ever so slightly.

"Safe?"

"Yeah. Safe." He placed his hands close to his mouth.

"Let me show you something."

Rene turned on the television and Nathan appeared on the screen, reading a document in a room, alone.

"The document you read here is about a fabricated, highly classified report that dealt with a mission in Egypt." Rene pointed to the document in Nathan's hands right before the next screen appeared. "Here, we placed you in a mock position with a set of role players to see whether or not you could properly conduct the task of talent spotting...recruiting others...students."

"Keep going." Nathan was focused on the television.

"You actually failed this task." Rene turned to look at Nathan. "One of the students was a female and she happened to be one of the role players intended to distract you."

"And she won?" Nathan pointed at a young woman dressed in a slutty gothic outfit, which included a plaid miniskirt.

"In one of your dreams, after this duration in the exercise, your subconscious showed us the poor decisions you made." Rene smirked. "Seems like you're the rough sex type of guy from what we saw."

"So I had sex with her?" Nathan's face grew red with embarrassment.

"In a bathroom stall, to be precise." Rene smiled and her cheeks reddened. "Need me to go on?"

Nathan's brows were knitted now. "Might as well."

Rene pulled out the DVD from the television and entered a new DVD. She hit the play button and then took a seat close to Nathan.

"What you are about to see is the most advanced, high-tech neurological imaging ever known to mankind." Rene leaned back. "We were capable of transferring your dreams into images and that is what you are about to see here."

"Wait a second." Nathan leaned forward and stood.

"What is it, Nathan?"

"Just wait for a moment." He hit the pause button on the DVD player.

"The girl...Her father was Sam, but I know him. He was in the hospital earlier. He said his name was Sexton." Nathan turned and looked at himself in a nearby mirror hanging on a wall.

"Yes. Sexton Colver." Rene pulled out a pen and began taking notes. "What about him?"

"I remember being in a car with him." Nathan turned and witnessed Rene taking the notes. "He tried to kidnap me. We were driving in a car. We went over a bridge. I killed him. Where did all that come from?"

"Nathan, when you were at Camp Dawson, one of your exercises was escape and evasion and high-risk capture. It happened right after the

Egypt exercise. You were tortured and part of that included being water-boarded, so you acted out in your dreams."

"I've been water-boarded before. What made this any different?" Nathan crossed his arms. "I've never reacted in the past based off my training the way I, if I understand, have been reacting recently. I'm a bit confused here."

"This was more advanced. The technique they used was…let's say…non-traditional." Rene didn't look at Nathan as she spoke. She was too busy taking notes. "They didn't care if you passed out. In fact, they wanted you to pass out. And we monitored your brain then as well."

"So none of it was real?"

Rene shook her head side to side.

"Let me tell you what is real, though." Rene tapped the end of her pen. "Perception."

"Perception?"

"Yes, perception." Rene stood and looked out a window. "Why is it that if the police interviews four witnesses about a car accident, more often than not, all four persons will claim they saw different things than the others?"

"No clue." Nathan walked toward the kitchen, turned on the faucet, and then placed his mouth under it to get some water. "But I'm sure you'll tell me, won't you?"

"Morals and values make up a large part of our culture." Rene turned away from the window and her all-black silhouette appeared as the sunlight surrounded her body's outline. "It is our culture that influences our daily perceptions."

"So what does this have to do with me or with what I've been through?"

"We gave you a vaccination. A powerful vaccination that is not known to the public." Rene walked away from the window and her features started to emerge under the light in the room. "The vaccination allows you to go anywhere in the world and will assist you in fighting off any diseases or biological dangers you may face, like malaria, polio, H1N1, etc."

"So I'm your guinea pig, huh?"

"If it makes you feel any better, from a medical research standpoint, your results were fascinating." Rene turned the DVD back on. "Do you remember any of this in your dreams?"

"This was me in Afghanistan." Nathan stared at the television. "Why are you showing me this?"

"You called in an airstrike. Do you remember?"

"Yes."

"Do you remember what happened after that?"

Nathan turned and looked at Rene with his eyes wide.

"The team you were assigned with conducted their battle-damage assessment. They searched the bodies of the dead. They did everything they were supposed to do." Rene pointed at the men on the television.

"And?"

"Keep watching." Rene watched along with Nathan as the men moved on from battle-damage assessments to inhumane war crimes.

"This isn't what happened." Nathan placed his hand over his mouth in shock. "They didn't commit any war crimes. How did you guys modify this? How did you guys get any of this on tape?"

"You gave it to us."

"Through my dreams." Nathan turned and looked at Rene.

"Precisely." Rene placed her hand on Nathan's elbow. "After your vaccination, that night, this is the one thing you dreamt about. Your subconscious manipulated what actually happened. And we just cannot seem to understand why your subconscious allowed you to believe the team on the ground did these heinous acts."

"Wait a second." Nathan placed his hands on Rene's arms and confronted her. "Earlier, you said I failed. And so far, based off everything you revealed, it seems like I failed everything through my subconscious, which your people were assessing. So if I failed everything, why would this Sexton guy say I passed?"

"That's something you will have to ask him." Rene looked down toward her arms, feeling Nathan's grip. "I am just a doctor, Nathan. I only know what I know from the medical…the neurological side of things. Sexton overseas the entire program, though."

"And you trust him?"

Rene tried to back away from Nathan, but his grip was too strong and fear grew in her. "No, I don't."

"Then why?" Nathan eased his grip. "Why do you work for him?"

"It's my job."

"A job where you don't trust those in charge?" Nathan stepped back. "So you know this job is unethical, but you stay because it's a job nonetheless. Isn't that right?"

Rene dropped her head in shame.

"I know why he said I passed even though I failed so many of the tests."

"What do you mean?" Rene lifted her head and looked at Nathan.

"I won because they couldn't take my conscious away from me." Nathan was looking around the room, in thought. "They tried, you tried, Sexton tried, but they failed. Everyone failed. Everyone but me."

"I think you're right, Nathan." Rene half-heartedly smiled. "Everyone failed but you."

Nathan looked down to the floor then began to walk through the room as if he were searching it. But what he was searching for may not have existed. The truth.

"Nathan, I'll be back." Rene looked down at her watch. "I need to go to a meeting, but I will return immediately after it's over."

"A meeting about me?"

Rene nodded.

"Don't bring any of them back here." Nathan pointed at Rene. "None of them. Including Sexton."

She didn't take her eyes away from his. "I need to go."

•••

Nathan was alone in the temporary quarters. After several minutes of sitting on the sofa, he quickly startled himself and began searching the home. It had been completely sanitized, meaning, nothing in it could pose danger. No kitchen knives, no extension cords, just a set of sheets that could be used as rope were he to need it.

I need to get the hell out of here. He continued to search the home. Out of the corner of his eye he spotted a micro camera tucked between the ceiling and a wall. *They have been recording everything. You mother fuckers!*

Glass. Find some glass, damn it!

Nathan rushed toward the mirror he had previously used to look at himself when speaking with Rene. He grabbed it off the wall and slammed it onto the floor, hoping a few pieces would separate. The shards were too large. He stomped on one of the pieces, making it smaller and more usable.

This is going to hurt. He grabbed one of the smaller pieces. *Suck up the pain, Nathan…Suck up the pain.*

He sat on the sofa and used the piece of mirror to cut the top of his hand. He cut deeper and clinched his teeth. *Get it out. Hurry, Nathan. Get it out of you.*

With the incision made, Nathan squeezed the skin on top of his hand. Enough pressure resulted so that the tracking device bubbled up out of his body.

Now move!

Before Nathan could leave the home, a subtle knock came from the front door.

"Nathan." A familiar voice said. "It's me, Rene. Can you let me in?"

"Thought you had a meeting." Nathan opened the door and blood trickled down his fingers.

"I left my office keys on the table."

"Bullshit!" Nathan grabbed Rene by her shirt and rushed her inside. "You knew what was going on. They told you to hurry back here."

"What are you talking about?" Rene looked down at the blood seeping from Nathan's hand. "What did you do? Nathan, talk to me. What are you doing?"

"They have been watching me. They have been watching us." Nathan pointed to the camera. "You said it yourself. Everything I've been doing has been closely monitored."

"Nathan, that's a security camera." Rene stepped away and her mouth opened as she gasped for air.

"Fuck you, Rene!" Nathan grabbed her neck.

"Let go of me…Please." Her eyes widened. "I am here to help you…Let me help you."

"Look what you're part of!" Nathan screamed. "You said you don't trust these people, yet you work for them, and now you want to help me?"

"Please, Nathan. Let go."

With the broken piece of mirror still in hand, Nathan released Rene and quickly trapped her in front of him in a choke hold. He raised the shard to the side of her neck, close to her carotid artery.

"One by one I am going to kill all of you."

"Nathan, I can help you." Rene pleaded. "Tell me what you want to know, and I will answer everything. Let me help you."

"You have a phone on you?" Nathan eased his grip and began to search her for a cell phone. "Call him. Get Sexton over here. Call him over the speaker phone."

"Let's talk first."

"We've done enough of that." Nathan pointed the jagged piece of broken mirror at Rene's face. "We're done talking. You and your team wanted to create a monster, well now you have him."

Rene quickly dialed Sexton Colver's phone number.

"Sexton, I need you here now." Rene eyed Nathan fearfully. "Urgently, I need you at the General's Palace. *Now*."

"I'm on my way." Sexton's concerned voice carried through the phone's speaker to Nathan.

"The General's Palace?" Nathan snickered. "That's your code, isn't it? A sign of duress?"

"Nathan, you're paranoid. I didn't say any code," Rene stressed. She closed her phone. "You're right. This program isn't for you. Let me speak with Sexton. He can remove you from it."

"So top secret…so highly classified…How do you remove someone from a program like this after they know so much about it?"

"Nathan…" Rene shed a tear out of fright. "I promise you, I can have you removed then you can go back into the civilian world. If that's what you want. I promise, we can make that happen. No one will hurt you."

"Of course no one will hurt me." Nathan peeked through a nearby window, awaiting Sexton's arrival. "People can't hurt me. Remember, your people made me into something special. You taught me special skills…the skills of a killer."

Sirens materialized in the distance.

"You lied to me." Nathan rushed toward Rene. "You fucking lied. You said you didn't give a duress code when you spoke with him. If that's true, why are the cops coming?"

"Nathan, Sexton knows what he's dealing with." Rene positioned herself across a table, away from Nathan. "He knows if I needed him here right away, something went terribly wrong. That's why the cops are coming."

"He knows what he's dealing with?" Nathan threw the table across the room and stalked toward Rene. "I am not a *what*! I am a *who*! A person. I am a fucking person with a God damn conscious!"

A sudden pounding struck the door. Rene and Nathan both looked at the door then quickly at one another. Nathan grabbed Rene by her shirt and brought her in closely, forcing her to her knees. He then knelt behind her.

"Don't do this." Rene tried to squirm, but to no avail. "You don't have to do this…Please."

"Shut up!" With one hand he placed the piece of mirror between her legs, close to her groin. With the other, he covered her mouth.

The door opened. Sexton appeared, behind him, two base police officers with weapons already drawn by their sides.

"Let her go." Sexton reached out his hand. "Let her go."

"Fuck you, Sam."

"My name is Sexton Colver. I am your handler." Sexton took a step closer. "You have a problem…I assure you it isn't with Rene. It's with me. Now let her go."

"She's part of your program." Nathan gritted his teeth and slowly inserted the mirror into Rene's femoral artery. "Like you, she doesn't deserve to live."

The police raised their weapons as they heard Rene's violent scream, which Nathan muffled with his hand. Sexton was quick to protest.

"I run this show." Sexton hollered at the officers. "Lower your weapons."

"Sir!" one of the police officers blurted.

"I said, lower your weapons!" Sexton demanded.

"You should have them kill me." Nathan maintained his position with his hand over Rene's mouth, to buffer the sounds of her agony. "One by one, I will take you all out. And it will be just as painful as what she is going through…more painful!"

"You want to kill me, son?" Sexton walked toward Nathan. "Then kill me. But let her go."

"Viper 1 to station," one of the police officers called into his radio. "I need ambulatory here, ASAP."

"Let her go, Nathan." Sexton took another step, as did one of the officers.

"What did he just say?" Nathan squinted at the officer. "Viper 1?"

"Let her go!" Sexton extended his hand.

"You want her?" Nathan asked as he slowly stood to both feet. "Take her."

Woozy from the loss of blood, Rene fell face-first to the ground. The police officer closest to Sexton dropped to a knee, checking her vitals. Nathan was quick to single-handedly twist the weapon out of his hand. The police officer who had called on the radio raised his weapon and pointed it at Nathan.

"Drop the fucking gun," the law enforcement officer screamed.

"Drop the gun, Nathan." Sexton stepped between Nathan and the cop who had the draw on Nathan. "Drop the gun, son."

"Fuck you, Sexton." Nathan squeezed the trigger, exploding a round through the barrel and into Sexton's chest.

Another shot ripped through the air, and Nathan fell to the ground.

"Viper 1 to station." The cop maintained his aim on a motionless Nathan Belovich. "I have three down."

The cop whom Nathan had previously disarmed checked Sexton's vitals then shook his head.

"Viper 1 to station." The cop walked closer to Nathan and kicked the gun he had used on Sexton away from his hand. "I have one KIA and two in critical."

A team of medics inserted Sexton's body into a black bag and zipped it closed for escort. Nathan watched as Sexton's body was escorted out of the home. He smiled, knowing his nightmare was one step closer to being over.

•••

Nathan Belovich stood at the counter. The man across from him placed a white paper bag with several brown bottles filled with pills next to the register. Few stood near the pharmacy pick-up line. Nathan didn't grab the bag. He just stood for a moment and looked at the contents within.

"Sleeping pills, anti-anxiety, anti-psychosis—you name it." Nathan continued to look at the bottles within. "It's all there and none of it seems to work."

"Mr. Belovich, if these drugs aren't working for you, I suggest you go back to your doctor and let him know." The pharmacist leaned his elbows on the counter. "Are you having bad reactions to these? Do you have any questions about these drugs? If so, I might be able to answer them."

"These drugs are supposed to help me." Nathan pulled out one of the bottles, a sleeping aid. "But why, for example, does this pill, which is supposed to make me sleep, actually give me nightmares that force me to wake in the middle of the night?"

"It's one of the side effects."

"This one…this is supposed to be anti-psychosis." Nathan pulled out another bottle. "Why does this one give me hallucinations in the middle of the day?"

"Again, it's one of the side effects."

"And this one?" Nathan pulled out another bottle. "What are the side effects of this one? Paranoia?"

"Mr. Belovich, go back to your doctor and tell him they aren't working." The pharmacist looked at the bottles on the counter. "As your pharmacist, I am concerned about what you are telling me. You need to go back to your doctor."

"Why should I trust my doctor?" Nathan pulled out the last bottle in the bag. "Aren't doctors supposed to be smart enough to not prescribe lethal concoctions?"

"They make mistakes." The pharmacist placed the bottles back in the bag.

Nathan swiped the bag from the pharmacist's hands. He threw the containers on the floor.

"I'm sorry." Nathan rushed to the bottles scattered by his feet. "I'm so sorry."

He saw a hand out of the corner of his eye. The fingers were manly, thick skinned with dirt under the nails. Nathan turned to see who was helping him.

"Seems you dropped these." The elder man wore a Marine Corps ball cap.

"Thank you, sir." Nathan took the bottle.

"Sir?" The man looked puzzled. "I haven't been called *Sir* in a while. You military?"

"Was."

"I served in Nam." The elder man smiled, knowing he was in the presence of a fellow American warrior. "Scout sniper. Name is Sean. Sean Attinger. I have a son in Afghanistan right now serving in Recon."

A tear trickled from Nathan's eye. It was uncontrollable.

"I'm sorry," Nathan said, wiping the wetness from his eye.

"For what?" Sean asked with a frown. "For what, son? What are you sorry about?"

"I…" Nathan shook his head. "I don't know."

"You have nothing to be sorry about." Sean wrapped his arm around Nathan.

Nathan, like a child who had lost all control, wept. His head was tucked deep into Sean's chest. Sean placed his hand on the back of Nathan's head and allowed the younger of the two to release his emotions.

"You have family, son?" The man placed his hands on Nathan's shoulders. "You have someone to speak to?"

"He has been living on the streets for several months," the pharmacist interjected.

"Homeless?" The man looked at the pharmacist who nodded in return.

Nathan stood in silence.

"Can't hold a job, wife left him. He has nothing." The pharmacist pushed a box of tissues closer to the men.

"And the government decided the best thing to do was prescribe him all these drugs?" Sean looked at the paper bag. "They never learned from when me and my guys came home. These drugs don't help anyone but the damn pharmaceutical companies and their politicians."

"C'mon, Sean." The pharmacist smiled. "Drugs help many people, and you know that. That's why you are here right now. Picking up your cholesterol medicine, aren't you?"

"Nathan, I have been involved in PTSD research ever since I was diagnosed almost forty years ago." Sean turned his back on the pharmacist. "I have some property…a farm…I want you to come with me. Let me help you."

"Sean, what are you doing?" the pharmacist asked.

"Getting him off these neurotoxic killers."

"Nathan, come with me." Sean placed his hand out for Nathan. "From one vet to another, together, we can get you back on your feet."

"How?" Nathan asked.

"Come with me and I will show you."

"How do I know I can trust you?" Nathan pulled away.

A young woman appeared. Her hair was long and brown. Her smile was warm.

"Dad, what are you doing?" she asked. "I was getting worried about you. You've been in here a while now. Everything all right?"

"Carol, this is my new friend…" Sean turned and looked at Nathan. "I'm sorry, I never got your name."

"Nathan. Nathan Belovich."

"Nathan, this is my daughter-in-law…Carol." Sean pointed at the young woman. "She's married to my son, Jack. He's the one I was telling you about who is deployed right now in Afghanistan."

"You have a good father-in-law." Nathan shook Carol's hand. "Thank you for your service."

"I'm not the one serving." Carol blushed. "That's my husband."

"You stand by his side, though," Nathan explained. "And you stand by the side of his entire family."

"Old Sean here took me in as his own daughter," Carol said as she placed an arm around her father-in-law. "I actually met his son on their farm. The family took to me I guess."

"You were working on the farm?" Nathan asked.

"No. I was visiting." Carol smiled at her father. "I went there after my last deployment."

"So you did serve?"

"I did. I was a nurse for the Army…I saw a lot…Someone suggested Sean's project to help me deal with PTSD, so I gave it a try."

Nathan smiled.

"Nathan…" Carol looked at the counter. "Would you like to come with us up to the farm?"

Nathan paused. He looked at the counter where the bag of prescription drugs rested then to Sean and Carol. He began to cry again. His body felt weak and his legs buckled from below, forcing him to the ground.

"I need to go to the farm," Nathan muttered with his hands covering his face. "I just want this to be over. Please, help this all end."

"Get up, son." Sean reached to help Nathan up. "This first thing you need to do is get back on your own two feet."

"How?" Nathan stood while looking into Sean's face. "How can I?"

"You just did."

Visit Kerry-Patton.com

Made in the USA
San Bernardino, CA
06 February 2014